"There's a really don't know anyt or the life we shared together other than the fact that I know it was brief."

"Well, then, you need to clue me in because I have no idea how you could forget the fact that you never lived in this house. You looked at Laurel like you've never seen her before and yet the two of you used to work side by side and talk for hours."

"I'm sorry. I'm seeing how difficult all of this is for you—"

"You can spare me your sympathy, Autumn. Just tell me the truth."

"Well, then, let's start right there. My name is not Autumn." She held up the necklace and took a step toward him, noticing how the grooves in his forehead deepened. "My name is Summer."

"You lied to me?" He gripped the edge of the counter like he needed to ground himself.

"No, I didn't. I've never met you before in my life. You were married to my identical twin sister."

TEXAS TARGET

USA TODAY Bestselling Author
BARB HAN

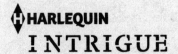

All my love to Brandon, Jacob and Tori,
the three great loves of my life.

To Babe, my hero, for being my greatest love and my place
to call home.

To my mom, you're almost there and you got this!

I love you all.

INTRIGUE

Recycling programs
for this product may
not exist in your area.

ISBN-13: 978-1-335-13682-4

Texas Target

Copyright © 2020 by Barb Han

For questions and comments about the quality of this book,
please contact us at CustomerService@Harlequin.com.

Harlequin Enterprises ULC
22 Adelaide St. West, 40th Floor
Toronto, Ontario M5H 4E3, Canada
www.Harlequin.com

Printed in U.S.A.

USA TODAY bestselling author **Barb Han** lives in north Texas with her very own hero-worthy husband, three beautiful children, a spunky golden retriever/standard poodle mix and too many books in her to-read pile. In her downtime, she plays video games and spends much of her time on or around a basketball court. She loves interacting with readers and is grateful for their support. You can reach her at barbhan.com.

Books by Barb Han

Harlequin Intrigue

An O'Connor Family Mystery

Texas Kidnapping
Texas Target

Rushing Creek Crime Spree

Cornered at Christmas
Ransom at Christmas
Ambushed at Christmas
What She Did
What She Knew
What She Saw

Crisis: Cattle Barge

Sudden Setup
Endangered Heiress
Texas Grit
Kidnapped at Christmas
Murder and Mistletoe
Bulletproof Christmas

Cattlemen Crime Club

Stockyard Snatching
Delivering Justice
One Tough Texan
Texas-Sized Trouble
Texas Witness
Texas Showdown

Harlequin Intrigue Noir

Atomic Beauty

Visit the Author Profile page at Harlequin.com.

CAST OF CHARACTERS

Summer Grayson—She's on a mission to find out what really happened to her twin sister, if she can stay alive.

Dawson O'Connor—This US marshal will do anything to talk sense into the woman he believes to be his ex, even if it puts his life on the line.

Jasper Holden—He worked at the coffee shop that connects the victims at the time of the murders but where is he now?

Mateus Hank—How does this wealthy banker fit into the picture?

Sean Menendez—Was this creepy maintenance worker fixated on one of the victims?

Drake Yarnell—He's a jealous ex but is he capable of murder?

Chapter One

The sun blasted on what had turned into a pavement melting summer day in Austin. Texas was legendary for its August heat. This day was going to be one for the books. Despite the triple-digit temperatures, navigating Congress Avenue still felt like running through a horde. Summer Grayson didn't have time to care about the sweat literally pouring down the sides of her face and dripping onto her shirt. She didn't have time to register how dry her mouth already was or how great a drink of water would feel right then. All she could care about was breaking free from the men who were right behind her, gaining ground with every step as she darted through throngs of people.

There were two men behind her. Their eyes trained on her. *She* was their target. No matter how much she desperately wanted to escape, to live, those men had other plans. Were these the same men who'd made her sister disappear?

Summer should never have pretended to be her identical twin, Autumn. Rolling the dice and claiming to be Autumn was backfiring big-time. On a base level, she'd needed to know if there was any possibility her sister was still alive even though she knew in her heart it wasn't likely. Criminal investigations took months, sometimes years. In too many cases, the criminal was never found. After two months of her own investigation, she'd been no closer to finding answers than when she'd first started.

So, yeah, she'd decided to cut corners and step into her sister's shoes. Getting desperate for answers had caused Summer to make mistakes that put these jerks on her tail. Risking a glance behind her added another miscalculation to the growing list. It slowed her down enough for one of the men to gain more ground.

The closest guy was the shorter of the two. He had light blond hair, a tan and a swimmer's build. His long torso and shorter legs were clad head to toe in black. He was also the faster runner of the pair. He was quick and lean, his face set in a permanent scowl. Everything about him said he was scrappy. The other jerk was at least six inches taller and thick. Thick neck. Thick arms. Thick hands.

Summer picked up the pace and risked another glance behind her, tamping down the panic that had adrenaline bursts fueling her legs. Scrappy was gaining on her and his friend, Thick Guy, wasn't far behind. No matter how hard she pushed her legs she wouldn't be fast enough to get away from Scrappy. Repeating a protection prayer that she'd learned as a young child, she pushed harder against burning thighs. It would take a miracle to get away.

No such marvel came. He caught hold of her. His grasp nearly crushed her bones. Icy fingers gripped her spine at the thought she would never know what had happened to her sister. As his nails dug into her skin, fear slapped her into realizing she might just end up in the same position. Gone.

A little voice in the back of her head picked that time to remind her how strong she really was. Despite being born prematurely and a minute later than her stronger, more athletic sister, Summer had enough fight in her to keep going despite the odds. Determination reminded her she'd survived then and would now, dammit.

Pushing harder, her thighs burned and her lungs clawed for air. She kept her pace, doing her level best to jerk her arm free. Giving in to pain could land her in a grave beside her twin sister, and she was certain that Autumn was dead. That was the only explanation for her sister's sudden disappearance. Granted, her sister had distanced herself from everything and everyone in the small town where they'd grown up years ago. She'd moved away from the Austin suburb and never looked back. Until recently.

Shutting out the past had been Autumn's way of surviving it—a past she'd refused to talk about even with her twin. Summer understood her sister's need for silence on a basic level, except for the part about closing off their relationship. The bond between twins was supposed to be ironclad. But Autumn was a grown woman capable of making her own decisions and Summer had no choice but to respect them.

Even so, no matter how rough it got for Autumn or how much time had passed in between communication, she'd always returned a 9-1-1 text from Summer.

"How are you still alive?" Scrappy's voice came out in a growl as he tightened the vise around her upper arm.

Those words nearly gutted Summer. Her sister had been secretive for the past couple years and had only touched base a few precious times. There wasn't a scenario where Autumn was alive that included her going dark. Summer's gut instincts said her sister was gone but if there was a shred of hope that Autumn was out there, alive, there was no end to the lengths that Summer would go to find her. Hell would have to freeze over before she stopped looking.

And if her sister was dead, the same went for finding justice.

This jerk wasn't going to stop her from finding the truth no matter how tight his grip became. More of that Grayson resolve that had kept Summer alive through more situations than she could count kicked into high gear.

"Last time I checked hell hadn't frozen over." Summer jerked her arm as Scrappy caught her by the other elbow. She had about two seconds to react before he dug his bony fingers into her arms. All that came to mind was what she'd learned in second grade and it basically only applied to a fire, but it was all she had. Stop. Drop. And roll.

So that's exactly what she did. On her way down, it dawned on her that smacking the concrete at a dead run was going to hurt. There was no choice but to push through the pain. Give up now and thick hands would close around her this time. She'd be hauled backward, landing hard on her backside and at the mercy of these two jerks.

This way, she could trip them and create a scene.

Stabs of pain shot through her calves as she tripped over her own feet and prepared to hit concrete. At least this way she could control the fall. That was the little white lie she told herself. She'd gotten good at letting herself believe the little lies that her sister had told her. Ones like, *I'm fine.* And, *All I need is a little more time to clear up some bad karma in Austin.*

Summer should have forced her sister to talk. She should have cornered Autumn and not let her walk away until she came clean about everything that was and had been going on in her life. When her sister had emailed to say that she'd found a wonderful man and that they'd gotten married, Summer shouldn't have left it at that. She shouldn't have taken Autumn at her word that all of life was suddenly smooth. *Smooth* and *Autumn* didn't belong in the same sentence. Eventually her past would catch up with her.

Her sister had gushed about her new husband, saying how strong he was and how protected she felt.

Looking back, Summer should've asked the question, *Protected from what?*

She could blame the fact that she'd been working two jobs to make ends meet. She could blame the fact that she was tired and not doing a heck of a great job managing her own life. She could blame her boss for keeping her late most nights. But the truth was that Autumn had always been a handful.

Until a year and a half ago when she'd announced the fact that she'd met *the one*. Learning that her sister had gotten married on a whim hadn't been the shock it should've been. Finding out she'd married into one of, if not *the* wealthiest cattle ranching families, had. Then again, Autumn had always managed to land on her feet.

Suspicion was second nature to Summer, who'd grown up watching over her shoulder for danger. And yet, her sister had sounded genuinely happy in her emails. That was something rare for a Grayson. And Summer had selfishly wanted a break from looking out for her sister. Autumn had a knack for placing herself straight-up in the middle of trouble. And trouble had a way of finding her. Like the time in high school when she'd made a pact with a star athlete on the soccer team to cheat off each other on a test. Adam Winston got caught and decided not to go down alone. He showed the principal his text exchange with Autumn. The funny thing was that Autumn had studied and could pass the test on her own merit. She'd played dumb because she thought he'd be more attracted to her.

As her shoulder hit the pavement, Summer unleashed a scream. She made the loudest noise that could come out of her mouth. The daytime crowd shuffled to get out of her way, like a sea parting. Summer realized the fall was going to be more than she expected, measured by the sheer number of gasps around her.

She did, however, elicit enough attention to make Scrappy think twice. In fact, his gnarly grip on her elbow released and he disappeared into the gathering crowd.

Summer's head smacked the ground harder than she'd anticipated. For a split second, she heard ringing in her ears. She could hop back up, but then what? The men would chase her again. This time, she might not be so lucky.

An authoritative female voice parted the crowd and a woman in uniform came into Summer's blurry vision.

"Ma'am, are you okay?" a female officer asked as she kneeled down.

"My name is Autumn Grayson and I need to confess to a crime."

The officer blinked shocked eyes at Summer. Those words seemed to grab her by the throat. "What was the offense, ma'am?"

The only thing that came to mind was the fire that had devastated a popular camping ground on the outskirts of Austin. It had been all over the news.

"Arson," she said.

"YOU'RE NOT GOING to believe who just confessed to arson." Dawson O'Connor's brother, Sheriff Colton

O'Connor, had been one hundred percent correct. Dawson couldn't believe that Autumn Grayson would confess to a crime there was no way she could've committed. Because he couldn't believe that his ex-wife could be capable of breaking the law. Not to mention the fact that she was scared to death of fire and would go nowhere near a campsite.

She'd been a city girl through and through. But then, he was still trying to believe that she'd served him divorce papers out of what felt like nowhere last year.

As far as he'd known, their marriage could have been saved. He wasn't the giving-up-when-times-got-tough kind. So, he'd been all kinds of surprised when he found out she hadn't taken their vows as seriously as he had. The note she'd left said she'd made a mistake, not to look for her, and he should forget he'd ever met her.

How was he supposed to do that? He'd been fool enough to spend time with her, marry her. And then he was supposed to…what? Forget any of that had ever happened? Far be it from him to dwell on unhappiness. Heaven knew he'd seen the effects of not being able to let go of a painful past firsthand in his own family. He had a wonderful mother who'd never really recovered from the night her firstborn child had been kidnapped in her own crib decades ago.

Dawson had had a sideline view to real tragedy. His mother had picked herself up and moved on best she could, always reminding her six O'Connor sons about the sister they never had the privilege to know.

Granted, getting a divorce was nowhere near the tragedy of losing a child and, worse yet, never knowing what had truly happened or if the child was alive. He chided himself for still hanging on to the pain of mistakenly falling for the wrong person. That was more a bad decision than a tragedy.

What was worse? He couldn't believe that he was sitting in the parking lot of the Travis County Jail with a handful of jewelry pieces in a box that his wife—correction *ex*-wife—had told him were family heirlooms. He'd had the sense from her that she hadn't grown up with much when it came to money or family. But then the subject of family had been off-limits. It should've been his first sign something was wrong.

He also shouldn't care about returning the pieces to her.

As a matter of principle, he didn't feel right holding on to them. Since she'd cut off all contact last year, he hadn't had an opportunity to hand them over. Call it cowboy code but he didn't like the thought of keeping someone else's belongings.

Engine idling. Hand on the gearshift. Foot on the brake. Time to make a decision. Drive away or go inside?

Dawson muttered a curse under his breath and shut off the engine. He made the trek into the jail and walked directly toward the officer at the counter.

"I'm here to see my wi—" He stopped himself right there. "Someone in your holding cell. Her name is Autumn Grayson." Since inmates in a holding tank weren't allowed visitors, Dawson pulled out his badge. Professional courtesy might get him through the steel doors. "My name is Marshal Dawson O'Connor."

The jailor perked up, his eyes widening for a split second. He extended his hand. "Nice to meet you, sir."

"The pleasure is all mine." He gave a small smile. "Is there any chance I can have a short visit with Ms. Grayson."

"Yes, sir." The cop examined the US Marshals badge on the counter in front of him as Dawson pulled a coin from his pocket. It was a custom that started long ago to give out a department-stamped coin when visiting a cooperating agency.

"Are you picking her up? The crime she confessed to committing has already been solved."

"We'll see." He doubted she'd go with him voluntarily.

The jailor introduced himself and took the offering with a broad smile. The tall, thin man who wore a white Stetson nodded his approval. "I appreciate this." He tossed the coin in the air, caught it and then said, "You want to follow me?"

It was more statement than question and didn't require an answer. Dawson followed. He was led into a small room with a table, two chairs opposite each other and a pair of doors. There was one behind him and one in front of him.

"If you'll take a seat, sir, I'll bring Ms. Grayson." With a nod, the officer left the room.

Sitting in the interview room, it dawned on Dawson just how much trouble Autumn might be in. She had, after all, confessed to arson. The who, how and why remained to be seen. He would ask routine questions and try to determine why she would volunteer to be charged for a crime she didn't commit.

There had to be more to the story, and he intended to get to the bottom of it. His mind snapped to self-defense. She was a beautiful woman who might've gotten involved in a bad situation. It happened.

Nothing could prepare him for the shot he took to the heart at seeing her again. She had changed a lot in the past year. Her shiny wheat-colored hair fell well past her shoulders in waves. Even with her eyes cast down to the white tiled flooring, he could almost see their violet hue. Her lips seemed fuller, pinker. Maybe it was the fact she had on no makeup and her hair looked natural, but this didn't seem like Autumn at all.

Maybe too much time had passed, and he wasn't remembering her very well. They'd had a whirlwind courtship before an even faster wedding.

She'd gained a few curves that made her even sexier. Hell, he didn't need to be thinking about those right now. He took in other differences, too. She no longer had bangs or wore designer clothing from head to toe.

Of course, those were cosmetic changes. He knew firsthand how a few little changes could make a person look completely different. He'd hidden enough witnesses in his day to know the value of a hat, scarf and pair of sunglasses.

Still, it struck him as odd that she wouldn't want to make eye contact with him. She had to know who was waiting in the room to talk to her. She would've been given the name of her visitor and even if she hadn't, that would give her even more reason to want to find out who would be sitting in the chair across the table from her.

Keeping her eyes cast down made her look guilty of something.

He cleared his throat and when she finally did glance up, the fear in her eyes was a second punch. What was she so afraid of? Him? Of his reaction to her walking out with no real explanation? He'd nursed a bruised ego longer than he cared to admit.

Dawson waited until the jailor instructed her to sit and then moved to the corner. Arms folded across his chest and feet apart in an athletic stance, he waited.

Autumn didn't sit. She stared at Dawson for a long moment and didn't speak, like they were playing a game and the person who spoke first lost. Her cheeks flushed, a telltale sign her body still reacted to him whether she wanted to admit it or not. Physical attraction had never been their problem. There was something different about the way she stood that he couldn't quite pinpoint. The oddities were racking up.

Even so, seeing her was a lightning strike in the center of the chest.

"Go away. You shouldn't be here." Hearing her

voice again shouldn't send a shot of warmth through his heart.

"Really? Because I was about to say the same thing about you." He clasped his hands together on top of the table and leaned forward. "What's going on, Autumn?"

That question could go way back to their past but that wasn't what he was referring to right now.

"I don't know what you mean, and my life is none of your business." Her shoulders tensed and the lines on her forehead appeared like they did when she was concentrating. Her defensive posture spoke volumes about how she felt at seeing him again. He shouldn't have expected anything less. She'd been clear about her intentions when she'd walked out and then had divorce papers served.

Those violet eyes threw darts at him. "Why are you here?"

"I came to return a few things you left at the ranch and to see if I can help you get yourself out of this…" he glanced around "…mess."

"You don't care about me."

"That's where you're wrong, Autumn. I do care." He wanted to add that he wished like hell that he didn't. He'd known seeing her again was going to be hard on him. He just didn't know how bad it was going to get.

Chapter Two

"I'll sign whatever you need to let her go," Dawson said to the jailor who was standing quietly in the corner.

"You can't do that." Summer pushed off the desk and started pacing. Nothing prepared her for being in the same room with Dawson O'Connor. She'd recognized her sister's husband from the pictures Autumn had sent of their wedding day. There'd been two. One of the couple standing next to each other. Dawson's arm had been around the waist of his bride, who'd been dressed in all white. For some reason that one burned into Summer's memory. Could it have been the only time her sister had seemed remotely happy? And then there'd been one of Dawson that had been taken on the same day. His face was turned toward a wooded area. He didn't seem to care that a camera phone was aimed at him. He was strong, like the muscles-for-days type of body. But, it was his smile that struck her the most.

In the pictures, he'd been seriously good-looking. Tie loosened, top couple buttons on his shirt undone, he'd been leaning against a fence post looking all relaxed. Happy. Seeing him in person, she realized the snaps hadn't done him justice. There was a magnetism about him that drew her gaze and made it stick. His looks came through loud and clear on the digital files, but he was sinning-on-Sundays gorgeous in person.

"Like hell I can't. Just because we're divorced doesn't mean I can't help you."

Summer didn't bother to hide her shock. "Hold on. What did you just say?"

"I said I wanted to help—"

She waved her arms in the air, stopping him midsentence. "Not that part. We're divorced?"

A dark brow went up and she realized her mistake. Her sister never mentioned anything about a divorce.

Dawson O'Connor had that whole tall, dark and handsome bit nailed down. It was easy to see why Autumn would be attracted to a man like him. His rough, masculine voice traveled over Summer like warmth and sex appeal and temptation.

Summer folded her arms tightly across her chest. She turned toward the door. "I want to go back to my cell *now*."

"Go ahead and do that." There was something foreboding in Dawson's tone that stopped her in her tracks. "Call the cop over and have me kicked out of here. Then what? What's your next play?"

She didn't immediately answer, and he must've taken that as a sign she was hearing what he was saying and willing to keep listening.

He continued, "I sure hope you have a next move in mind because this one seems like an act of desperation."

She couldn't argue. She didn't have it in her to put up a fight. Plus, he was speaking the truth. In fact, no truer words had ever been spoken. She'd been desperate. Desperation caused her to pose as her sister. Desperation caused her to confess to a crime she didn't commit. The only reason she'd confessed was to escape the bad guys on her trail. And it was desperation that had her needing Dawson O'Connor to be as far away from her as possible.

And, no, she hadn't figured out her next move. Plus, she was starving. Her stomach growled, picking that time to remind her that she hadn't even figured out her next meal.

His tone softened when he said, "Allow me to get you out of here. We both know you didn't commit the crime you're confessing to and so do they. I don't know what you're up to and I don't know why this seemed like a good option." He waved his arms in the area. "Let's go somewhere we can talk and see if I can help you get back on your feet."

His unexpected kindness tapped into a long-forgotten place buried deep inside. A place that had no business seeing the light of day.

"I appreciate your willingness to help me after what I put you through." Summer had no personal knowledge of exactly what that meant but knowing her sister it was a lot. Based on the look in his eyes, it was far more than this man deserved. "I can't accept your help. We're divorced. What happens to me doesn't concern you anymore."

"Is that what you think? I'm the kind of person who could walk away from someone I cared about once? Because if that's true you clearly did us both a favor by walking out last year." He threw a hand up before she could answer. "Never mind. The past is the past. We both moved on. And now you find yourself here. You don't want my help. There's not a whole lot I can do about that. But let me ask you this. How long do you really think it's going to take for whomever you're running from to find you here?"

Those words were the equivalent of a bucket of ice water being dumped over her head. He was right. Hearing him say those words as plainly as he had brought home the fact that she wasn't safe anywhere anymore. The cops were onto her about the lie and she figured they'd boot her out soon anyway.

Autumn had gushed about life on the ranch. A remote location far away from Austin sounded pretty good right about now.

Summer took in a deep breath meant to fortify her nerves and prepared to shock him. "Fine. I'll let you pay my bail, but you have to take me home with you."

SUMMER WAS STILL surprised Dawson had agreed to her terms as she walked into his home on an expansive ranch property. Mental images of him sharing this place with her sister slammed into her—images she didn't like for reasons she didn't want to explore. An attraction was so out of the question.

She glanced around the room and was initially shocked to realize there were no photographs of the two of them. Then, it dawned on her that her sister had filed for divorce last year. Of course, any pictures that had been hanging on the walls would've been taken down.

The place was decorated in a surprisingly masculine style. Or, maybe it shouldn't be such a surprise. Again, he might've redecorated. Thinking her sister had walked in this very room not that long ago struck an emotional chord.

Summer tucked her chin to her chest and blinked her eyes, trying to clear away the tears threatening. For the sake of Autumn's memory, Summer needed to hold it together. For the sake of the investigation, she needed to continue the lie even though after meeting Dawson it was increasingly difficult to hold the line. For the sake of her own sanity, she needed to keep her distance from him on both an emotional and physical level.

Getting too close to her sister's ex would only add to both of their heartbreak. Despite the tough exterior, one look in his eyes told her that his feelings had run deep for Autumn.

A sound in the next room caused her to jump over the back of the couch and drop to her knees. It took a second to register the fact that Dawson's eyes were on her, studying her. Analyzing her.

Of course, she should've realized her extreme reaction would draw his attention. She also shouldn't let it warm her heart that Dawson still cared enough about her sister to drive all the way to Austin to bail her out of jail.

"It's just Laurel. She's probably finishing up cleaning for the day." He didn't so much as blink.

"You have a housekeeper?" The raised eyebrow he gave her in response to her question told her she'd just made another mistake. She needed to keep the questions to a minimum. Lay low for a few hours until she could figure out her next move, grab a meal and definitely not talk to him more than she had to.

There was no way she would stick around and put Dawson or his family in danger. Was that the reason her sister had divorced him? Had she known trouble was coming and wanted to protect him? Cut all ties to save him from her fate? Had she married a US marshal thinking he could keep her safe?

"You know we did. I still do. Even though I've told Laurel a hundred times I don't need the help. She's stubborn that way. You remember that about her." From everything she could tell about the man so far, her sister was right. He was good-looking beyond a casual description. Carved-from-granite jawline. Check. Thick, dark hair—the kind that her fingers itched to get lost in. Check. Serious brown eyes with a hint of sadness. Check. He was kind. It was the only explanation for him going out of his way to help her after being served papers. He didn't seem like the kind of person who took divorce lightly. In fact, he seemed like the type who put family above all else.

A middle-aged woman padded into the room. She had a kind face and a stout build. In one hand, she white-knuckled the handle of a pail. In the other, she gripped a white cleaning rag.

Summer scrambled to her feet. The woman—Laurel—gasped. Her chin practically dropped to her chest. Mouth agape, she released her grip on the bucket. It tumbled onto the tile, crashing against the flooring.

"I'm sorry." Summer glanced around, desperate to find something to help contain the spill. She ran toward the open-concept kitchen and made it to the counter with the paper towel roll at the same time as Dawson.

He gave her a small look of approval, like she remembered something because she was home. That look nearly cracked her heart into two pieces. Getting out of there and out of Katy Gulch just jumped up her priority scale. She hadn't found paper towels because this was her home. Their location had been intuitive. They'd been placed next to the kitchen sink—an obvious place. All she'd done was follow a line across the counter until she saw the paper towels.

It dawned on her that Dawson must've loved her sister and the divorce had to have been hard on him. Autumn had ended their marriage without explanation or ceremony.

This close, she could easily see the dark circles cradling his honey-brown eyes. She could almost feel the toll that caring for Autumn had taken on him, because the feeling was so familiar to her it was palpable. Caring for Autumn was hard. Draining at times. Still the question burned. What had Autumn gotten herself into?

Happiness had always been fleeting for a Grayson. It was beyond Summer's comprehension how her sister could've found it with this man and then walked away. She grabbed the paper towels off the counter and turned toward the mess. In all the commotion, Summer didn't notice the small black-and-white dog that had run behind Dawson.

She dropped to the floor and used half the roll of paper towels, trying to mop up the spill.

Laurel smiled nervously at her. She had kind eyes and what Summer was certain would be an equally kind heart.

Dawson joined them, the little dog by his side, which she could now see was a puppy. Since the dog was probably a safe topic, Summer decided to start there.

"Who is this little guy?"

"My shadow," Dawson said. "Hence, his name is Shadow."

"You should've seen this little guy when Dawson first found him." Laurel made a tsk-tsk noise. "It's impossible to imagine what kind of person could just dump a little guy like this all alone in the country, leaving him unable to fend for himself."

"What happened?"

"Nothing," Dawson said, looking embarrassed by the attention. "He got into a tangle with something—"

"Dawson's being modest. Shadow was attacked

by a coyote. Dawson heard what was happening and hopped off Mabel—" she flashed eyes at Summer when no recognition dawned "—you remember his horse."

"Oh. Right. Mabel. Yes." Lying to this sweet woman made Summer feel awful. There was no way she could keep up the charade. Telling Laurel, exposing the truth, might just put the woman in danger. Summer couldn't do that, either. This woman was all s'mores and campfires and the kind of person who probably baked cookies on a chilly day.

"So, Dawson here literally forced open the jowls of the coyote and ripped this little guy from its teeth." Laurel was clearly proud of him, not that Summer could blame the woman. "Never mind that the coyote's mouth then closed on Dawson's elbow. Tore him up pretty good before he managed to get free."

Summer didn't notice his left elbow until then. A pretty gnarly scar ran a solid four inches across his skin.

"Wild things are dangerous. It was really brave of you to take on the coyote." She tried to stifle the admiration in her voice. It was difficult. She also realized the statement covered more than just his coyote encounter.

"Laurel is making too big of a deal out of what happened. All I know is that helping this little guy out of trouble gave me a shadow I can't shake around the house." He nodded toward the black-and-white pup that had yet to grow into his oversize paws. The hint of annoyance in his tone seemed clearly just for show. Dawson scratched the dog behind his ears.

If the little guy had been a cat, he would've purred. She could think of worse problems than to have the adoration of an adorable puppy. And Summer figured little doggies weren't the only things willing to follow Dawson O'Connor around, eyes filled with admiration. With sex appeal in buckets, she suspected half the women in town would do the same thing. The other half were either married or dead.

Summer also couldn't help but notice how Laurel kept a tentative eye on her. The kind housekeeper looked like she'd seen a ghost. Based on her expression and reactions, the woman Laurel assumed was Autumn was the last person she expected to see. More proof that Summer's sister had left a mess in her wake. Autumn could be like a volcano. Mesmerizing to see and experience until she erupted. Then, it was pure devastation for anyone who got too close or landed in her path.

"The mess is all cleaned up now. Can I drop Shadow off at the barn on my way to the main house?" Laurel asked.

"He'd like that. Wouldn't you, little guy?" Dawson picked up the pup in one sweeping motion and brought him nose to nose.

"Having another dog to play with might be good for him." Summer could've sworn the puppy smiled.

"He loves playing with Apollo and it's good for him since he lost Daisy. Apollo has been moping around for weeks. The only time I've seen him perk up in the slightest is when Shadow comes around." Laurel walked over to Dawson, who handed over the sweet pup.

"Be nice to Apollo. No biting his ears with those sharp puppy teeth." Despite the warning, his voice was low and warm as he scratched the pup behind the ears. "Will you let me know when I need to pick him up?"

"I sure will." Laurel excused herself before gathering her supplies and making a quick exit.

Lying to the woman with kind eyes about Summer's identity was the equivalent of a physical stab. Perfection had never been her goal and heaven knew she got into her fair share of troubles growing up. Being her own parent from an early age had a way of teaching with a baptism by fire. No one would ever accuse Summer of being perfect. But she was not a liar.

Honesty rated highly in her book. Autumn, on the other hand, had always claimed that bending the truth never hurt anyone. It wasn't true. Summer knew from personal experience how her sister's tiny white lies left marks on the inside—marks that weren't visible to the naked eye.

So, she seemed to find herself between a rock and a hard place as she pushed to standing. Being in close proximity to Dawson, close enough to smell his warm, masculine scent, wasn't helping with the guilt racking her.

"You've been really kind, and I appreciate it. Especially after the way you were treated." There was something very primal in her that could not take the blame for her sister's actions. Maybe it was because standing in the light of Dawson's honey-gold eyes made her want to be honest with him. An important part of that was being authentic.

But honesty at this point in the game would have a price. It was easy to see that a man like Dawson wouldn't walk away easily from someone who needed a hand up. He would see it as his duty to help just as he'd seen it as his responsibility to get her out of jail and talk sense into her.

"Do you mean after the way *you* treated me?" He seemed to regret those words the minute they came out of his mouth. "Don't answer that. Whatever happened between us is water under the bridge. The reason I came to see you today wasn't as altruistic as you might think." He walked over to the counter where he'd placed his keys and picked up a small box. She'd noticed it in his hands earlier but with everything going on didn't think to ask about it.

She walked over to the kitchen counter and placed her hands on it to steady herself.

"These belong to you. You said they were important." He set the box on the counter next to her and walked away. "I'm about to make coffee. Do you want a cup?"

"No coffee for me. But, thanks." She had no plans to stick around long enough to finish a cup.

Summer stared at the box like it was a bomb about to detonate. Did she even want to know what was inside? Sadness was a physical ache. Summer of all people knew that even though her sister could be selfish and focused on all the wrong things sometimes, Autumn had also been her best friend and partner in crime growing up. Autumn's faults could so easily have been Summer's considering the childhood they'd shared.

Life had hardened them both at too young of an age. Broken them? There'd been times when Summer wondered if her sister had been capable of caring for anyone but herself. She'd asked the question countless times, wondering if she was wasting her time and energy on someone who would always be a taker.

"Your stomach growled earlier. You're here. You may as well eat and have some coffee before you take off again." She didn't want to hear the twinge of hurt in Dawson's voice. Especially since he did a fine job of covering it with a cough.

Trying to find out what had happened to her sister was becoming an exercise in stupidity. So far, all she'd done was attract the attention of very bad people. People who wanted her dead. Maybe it was time to move on. It would be easy enough to change her appearance and disappear off the grid for a little while. Could she, though? Could she walk away without knowing what had happened to Autumn?

Summer tapped her finger on the lid of the small box. She wrapped her fingers around it, still unsure if she wanted to see what was inside.

Her fist tightened around the top of the box as she opened it, memories assaulting her. These few pieces of jewelry were her sister's most prized possessions? It was all junk, worth nothing when it came to money. Memories were a different story.

Her fingers closed around a tarnished chain. The necklace that spelled out one word brought back a treasure trove of memories from the county fair.

This was considered one of her sister's most prized possessions? Because the name on the necklace read *Summer*.

Chapter Three

Dawson watched as his ex-wife stood in his kitchen, tracing the letters on the necklace using her index finger. Autumn had changed. A thought struck that maybe she'd been in an accident and suffered some type of head trauma. She pretended to know the house even though she never lived in it. In fact, he'd moved in three months ago after some tweaks to the original plan—a plan she'd helped him design.

The two of them had made big plans to move into the home that she was going to decorate. He'd even started contemplating the next logical step, a family. But those plans had never gotten off the ground.

After working with the contractor to make enough changes for the house to feel like *his* and not *theirs*, he'd moved in. It only took a few phone calls and clicks to cancel all the furniture and decorations she'd ordered. The custom pieces had been finished and donated to the House of Hope for abused women and their children.

With the addition of oversize leather couches and

a large metal star hanging over the fireplace, the place had become home for the bachelor.

The twist of fate that brought Autumn into the space he never thought she'd see had him off-balance. He needed to stay focused. He poured a cup of coffee and took a couple of sips. It was time for answers.

"Why did you say you did it?" He started right in with one of the biggest.

She ducked her head, chin to chest. Her mannerisms were different from a year and a half ago. It was an odd sensation to be staring at a woman he'd known intimately and yet feel like he was staring at a total stranger now. Could the fact he was looking at his ex through a new lens be the impact of divorce?

"I was desperate." Well, now he felt like he was starting to get somewhere. He'd been beginning to think this wasn't Autumn at all, which was crazy because she looked exactly like her.

"Why?"

"Believe me when I say you really don't want to know." There was no conviction in those words. There was sadness in spades and a lost quality that caused a knot to form in his gut.

"Why not let me be the judge of that? I think I have a pretty good handle on what I do and do not want to know." That came out a little harsher than he'd intended. He tried to soften his tone when he said, "Believe it or not, I'd like to help."

"You can't. This is something I have to deal with

on my own." Now her intention came out loud and clear. Hurt and stubbornness laced her tone.

"Will you at least tell me why you have to deal with this by yourself?"

She shook her head and didn't make eye contact.

"Does this have anything to do with why you walked out on our relationship?" His bruised ego needed to know because that darn thing still licked his wounds.

"I didn't give you a reason?" This time, she made eye contact. Eyes wide with a look of disbelief caused more questions to form in his thoughts.

"No. But it's not too late. Tell me why. Your note didn't explain what went wrong. I thought we had a good thing going. Granted, looking back, it wasn't perfect, but we had a base to build on."

"I'm sorry. I can't do this with you right now." The hint of fear in her voice didn't get past him.

"Do what? Finally answer a question? Give me the real reason why you left our marriage after exchanging vows? In case you didn't notice, I took those seriously." He pushed even though he knew better. As a seasoned law enforcement officer, he had developed and honed instincts that told him he was doing nothing but backing her into a corner. Just like the coyote, she'd bite.

"I didn't deserve you." She broke eye contact and guilt stabbed at him. But guilt for what? Why was he suddenly feeling like a jerk for making her feel bad? She'd walked away from their marriage not the other way around. Losing the pregnancy had been even harder on her than it had on him, but he hadn't seen a need for a divorce despite that being the reason for the marriage in the first place.

Her admission struck a nerve. It was impossible, though, not to feel like he was forcing his help on her right now. She was in a desperate situation and he'd been pushing her to take his aid.

"It's not fair of me to put you in the position of explaining yourself. You didn't ask for me to show up today—"

"Which doesn't mean I'm not grateful you did." She had the necklace draped over her opened hand. Giving her back something that she so obviously cared about made him feel like maybe this day hadn't been a total mistake.

"It seems like you've gotten yourself into a situation that maybe you're having a hard time figuring out how to get out of. We've all been there—"

She clucked her tongue. "Somehow I doubt that. I can't imagine a man like you would know anything about regret."

Dawson stood there for a long moment, taking in her body language. Shoulders tensed, her feet aimed toward the back door, everything about her said she was in for a quick exit. It was his fool pride wanting answers from someone who so clearly didn't care about the marriage as much as he did. *Hadn't cared.* Past tense.

"Okay, let me try this another way." He motioned toward the sets of keys. They hung on a key rack nailed to the side cabinet near the hallway that led to the garage. "There are several vehicles in the garage. I'm sure it won't be too hard to figure out which key belongs to what vehicle. Take whatever you want. No questions asked. You don't have to worry about returning anything. I'm not bringing in the law."

"You are the law. And didn't you just post bail for me? Won't you get into trouble if I disappear?"

"My lawyer can tie up the courts for years until they forget all about my connection to you and technically all I did was sign paperwork to get you released. We both know you're innocent, Autumn." A strange look passed behind her eyes when he said her name. He didn't go into the fact that he'd put his reputation on the line to help her. "Tell me an amount and I can pretty much have as much money as you need at your disposal." He checked the clock hanging over the cabinets in the kitchen. "Bank is about to close." Of course, he could call up his banker at any moment and have the bank reopened for him. A selfish part of him wanted to stall for time, maybe wanted a little bit more time with Autumn before she disappeared again.

She just stood there, a blank look on her face. "You would do all that for me?"

He waved her comment off like it was nothing.

"Seriously?" She started pacing. "That's pretty much the nicest thing anyone's ever volunteered to do for me." She glanced up at him nervously. "I mean, there are so many nice things you did when we were married but I walked out on you."

His ex didn't seem to remember much about their

past. Had something happened? Trauma? Working the angle that she'd somehow lost her memory, he asked, "Really? You remember nice things I did for you? Name one."

"I-UH—" SUMMER DREW a blank. And then an obvious answer smacked her between the eyes. "You asked me to marry you."

His eyebrow shot up.

"And there were so many other things that it's hard to remember them all right now." She gripped her forehead, trying to stave off the massive headache forming in the backs of her eyes. Headaches were like that. They had a way of taking seed and then sprouting tentacles that seemed to wrap around her brain and squeeze.

"Did something happen to you, Autumn? Were you in some kind of accident?"

His questions registered. He thought she was suffering from some kind of brain trauma, which basically meant Autumn never told Dawson about her. It would be so easy to go along with that line, a quick escape out of an almost unbearable situation. But she couldn't go there. "No. I wasn't, Dawson."

"You've changed a lot in the past year and a half. More than I expected. I mean, you look like my ex-wife. There's no debating that. But it feels like I'm talking to a complete stranger. On the outside, it's you but you don't act like her. Her mannerisms are totally different. And I just thought there had to be an easy explanation."

She wanted to give him one. She wanted to help him make sense of a marriage that had been cut short. She wanted to give him answers he seemed to crave in order to go on with his life. He seemed like the kind of person who deserved that and so much more. But how without adding fuel to an already blazing fire?

If she came clean with him right then and there, it would only lead to more questions. Worse yet, he might want to get involved and end up hurt or dead. That would be on her conscience for the rest of her life.

"Money would be a huge help, but only as a loan. You have to promise to let me pay it back." She could use a cash infusion to keep her off the grid. The investigation had to be put on the back burner until the situation cooled off. She'd riled someone up. Maybe she could rent a cabin in the woods until life chilled out again.

"Done. How much do you need?"

"A couple thousand dollars if you can spare it." She almost winced saying the number out loud.

"I can do a whole lot better than that. Twenty-five thousand—"

"I'd never be able to pay that much back." She blinked at him, a little bit dumbfounded. Her sister had said the man she'd married came from a wealthy family. Summer couldn't even fathom someone who could conjure up that kind of cash on a moment's notice.

"You don't have to. It's yours already. Remember? I put it in your account when we got married and you never used it."

"Now I know you're lying." Or testing her. The latter made more sense.

"The money is sitting in your account. What you do with it is your own business." There was a sadness to his tone she didn't want to pick up on. She couldn't afford to care about his feelings right now, not when there was so much at stake. The fact she was aware that he tried to cover with a sharp edge to his tone made everything so much worse.

"You said I could borrow a vehicle..."

"Take whatever you need. There are several in the garage to choose from. You didn't take your own when you left—"

She was already shaking her head before he finished his sentence. "I'd like to borrow one of yours. Preferably something I've never driven before."

He'd mentioned that the bank was almost closed. They needed to hurry if she was going to get out of there. "Is there any chance we can make it into town tonight?"

"It's too late to go through normal procedures." He glanced away from her when he spoke. What was he hiding?

Summer ran through possibilities in her mind. She could take twenty-five thousand dollars in cash and disappear for a while. Then what?

Keep on running the rest of her life? She'd been living a lie recently and it was coming back to bite her. Would she turn out exactly like her sister? Lying and then covering up the lies. Could she convince herself it was all for the best? That the only reason she lied was to help other people? Could she walk away from investigating her sister's disappearance? Because if she did that, she wouldn't recognize herself anymore.

Staring at a pair of honest honey-brown eyes standing a few feet in front of her, she realized that she could never be the kind of person who could look into them and lie. That even little white lies meant to protect others ended up hurting them more than anything else.

Telling Dawson the truth was risky. It could put him in danger. Not telling him seemed like it could also put him in harm's way. Especially if he started digging around to figure out what was really going on.

Ignorance wasn't always bliss. Sometimes, it could kill.

She decided to clear up this whole mess by coming clean with him. He worked in law enforcement and he seemed to care about her sister. He would know how to protect himself if he was aware of a threat. When she really thought about it, he was a US marshal. Weren't they involved in witness protection? She personally had no idea.

"Dawson, I'm going to tell you something that you might not be ready to hear. You deserve to know the truth." Just saying those words caused her heart to hammer her rib cage.

He set his coffee cup down on the granite countertop and crossed his arms over his chest like he was bracing himself for the worst.

"I don't know much about your marriage except that I know you got married on the last day of January." She held her hand up to stop him from speaking before he could respond because she could already see the questions forming in his eyes. "I was honest before. I haven't been in an accident or had any kind of head trauma."

"Then, what?"

Speaking the words out loud was proving to be so much harder than saying them in her head. She was trying to think of a way to ease him into the news rather than blurt it out and completely shock him. "There's a really good reason why I don't know anything about this house or the life we shared together other than the fact that I know it was brief."

"Well then, you need to clue me in because I have no idea how you could forget the fact that you never lived in this house. You looked at Laurel like you've never seen her before and yet the two of you used to work side by side and talk for hours."

"I'm sorry. I'm seeing how difficult all of this is for you—"

"You can spare me your sympathy, Autumn. Just tell me the truth."

"Well then, let's start right there. My name is not Autumn." She held up the necklace and took a step toward him, noticing how the grooves in his forehead deepened. "My name is Summer."

"You lied to me?" He gripped the edge of the counter like he needed to ground himself.

"No, I didn't. I've never met you before in my life. You were married to my identical twin sister."

Chapter Four

Dawson studied the woman in front of him, trying to give his brain a minute to process what he'd just heard. He must've looked her up and down like she was crazy, because she put her hands up in the surrender position.

"I know how that must sound but it's true. I should probably be surprised that you don't know about me. In a normal family, we would. My sister kept secrets. We're identical twins and I absolutely know something happened to my sister. I tracked her to Austin where a pair of men found me. They said I wouldn't die and that they intended to finish the job." Those honest violet eyes blinked up at him and his heart stuttered. "If my sister was alive, I would've heard from her by now."

There were so many questions mounting. This one popped first. "I need to rewind for just a second. Your name is Summer, and I was married to your identical twin sister. You're here to find out what happened to your sister, who you believe is gone?"

She nodded. "I'm sorry to say this to you, because I know you lov—"

"Thing of the past." He cut her off right there. There was no use going down that road again.

"She is gone." Her chin quivered and she ducked her head to one side.

Summer's answer caused his chest to squeeze. He didn't have to have the same feelings for Autumn as he once did.

"How do you know?" Disbelief washed over him as he studied her for any signs she was lying. His brain couldn't process the news. More questions flooded him as his past unraveled. He narrowed his gaze and studied the woman in his kitchen. He'd noticed something different the second he saw her at county lockup.

"Hear me out. I've been living in Washington State where I work as a waitress. My sister and I always stay in touch."

"And yet I had no idea you existed," he said low and under his breath. Had she planned to leave all along?

"I'm sorry about that. I'm puzzled about that part as well because she told me about you. Granted, it was after you were married. We may go a while in between connecting but we always circle back. She'd been leaving cryptic messages lately about her past."

"A past you knew very little details about if I had to guess." A picture was emerging. Autumn would classify herself as a free spirit, forgetting all about the hurt and questions she left behind.

His comment seemed to offend Summer based on her deep frown lines. Hell, he hadn't meant to add to her hurt. It was obvious she cared about her sister or she wouldn't be here trying to find out the truth.

"My sister was far from perfect. No one knows that better than I do." She folded her arms across her chest and leaned back on her heels.

He was taking all this new information personally. How could he not? He'd met someone, had been told he was going to be a parent long before he was ready and with someone who he'd only known a handful of months.

Autumn had been good, though. When he'd popped the question, she said she had to think about it. Over the days that followed, she'd seemed genuinely anguished about the decision to rush their relationship and that had only made him want to protect her more.

How stupid was he?

Normally, liars gave themselves up. There were signs. The direction of their gaze when they responded to a question would tell him how truthful they were being. Or how fast a verbal response came. A liar paused in the wrong places. They were also good at hiding their eyes or mouth during questioning. There were other telltale signs like coughing or clearing their throat before answering.

A practiced liar could get around most of the signs. A pathological liar—someone who believed the lies—was the most difficult to detect.

Summer was a valuable witness and now that Pandora's box had been opened to his past, he needed answers. She was the fastest route and they both had the same goal.

"It'll take me a minute to get my head around this…situation. I don't take vows lightly and I'm currently in a tailspin, which doesn't mean I don't want to help. Please, continue."

Summer eyed him warily and his heart squeezed. Her pain was obvious. He wasn't the only one Autumn had hurt.

She took in a breath before her next words. "The last time I heard from her she said that she was going through something with an ex but not to worry. Everything was fine and she was happy with you."

He shot her a look but quickly apologized for it.

It was impossible to believe she ever cared about him, considering the fact she'd walked away without a backward glance. If she'd been in trouble, he couldn't think of a better person to help than a member of law enforcement. If she'd needed to hide, who better to ask than a US marshal? Relocating witnesses was one of his specialties.

"For what it's worth, I do think she loved you," Summer clarified.

Now he really shot her a look.

"What? You don't believe me?" she asked.

"No, I don't. How could anyone be happy who is living a lie? The woman I married told me she was an only child and that her parents were killed in a car crash on the interstate a few years after she went to college." He stopped right there because the woman's jaw looked like it was about to smack the floor. "Explain that."

"She doesn't like to talk about the past. It was hard

for both of us. I think there was a year in California where we got passed around to four different foster homes and there was this point where I saw it break my sister. I think she shut down some critical emotions and never could get them back. She wasn't a bad person. She was just..." Her gaze shifted up and to the right like she was searching for the right word.

"Lost?" The way Summer, if he could believe that was her name, spoke about Autumn made him realize she *did* know her sister. As identical twins, it stood to reason the two would have known each other intimately. "Why would she suddenly move to Texas if she grew up in California?"

"You want my best guess?"

He nodded.

"We're originally from here. Our parents were together when we were really young, and we lived in Austin as a family. Our dad took off when we were still little. My mom had a cousin in California. She thought she could make a better life for us there. She was a very beautiful woman and she felt like maybe there was easy money out there in Los Angeles as a model."

"But there wasn't?"

"LA was harder than she expected, and she got depressed. Four of us lived in a one-bedroom apartment and her cousin wasn't happy Mom wasn't pulling her weight. There were some parties in our apartment complex, and I remember coming home from school to find her passed out on the couch. Her drinking got out of control and she couldn't keep it together."

Again, this was something Dawson came across in his line of work more than he cared to. Despite his frustration at the situation, he had sympathy for Summer and Autumn. No kid deserved a father who turned his back on the family or a mother who couldn't cope with the demands of bringing up children. There were resources out there for those who would use them but it was always the kids who suffered and they were the innocent ones in the equation.

"Someone called child protective services when my sister and I were locked out of our house. Our mom got in a really bad fight with her boyfriend, so he pushed us outside and locked the door while he broke her nose and her jaw. I think our neighbors were afraid of what might happen to us next, so they called the authorities."

His heart broke for their lost childhood. It was obvious that Summer was Autumn's identical sister. Put the two of them facing each other and it would be like one of them looking into a mirror. But they seemed like exact opposites in terms of personality despite growing up under the same conditions.

What he couldn't figure out was why his wife would lie to him. In fact, their entire life was built on lies. More of that anger and frustration built up inside of him.

"Autumn was in trouble based on the texts. What makes you think she's gone?" He couldn't imagine a scenario where this would be Autumn standing in front of him.

"She stopped all communication. She never would

have done that." Summer seemed convinced on that point. Dawson couldn't say one way or the other. He should've known his wife better than that. Autumn had shown up in his life and tore through town, his heart, like a tornado.

"With all due respect, she married a man who never knew you existed," he countered.

"I see your point." She was rocking her head. "But I have known my sister for the past twenty-nine years. Even when she spirals, she answers my texts. And especially our emergency signal."

Well she obviously knew her sister a hell of a lot better than he'd known his wife. Had she been in real trouble? Was that the reason she'd taken off?

Dawson's mind was still spinning. He couldn't help but think he'd been taken for a fool. The unproductive thought wouldn't help matters.

He wasn't in love with her anymore. That ship had sailed. Lick his wounds? He'd done that. Being burned had a way of bruising the ego.

As weeks had turned into months with no word from Autumn after divorce papers had been signed, he realized his mistake had been marrying someone he barely knew.

There were other things that she told him and he now wondered if there was any truth to her words.

"Can I ask you a question?" Dawson wasn't exactly sure he wanted to know the answer.

She shrugged. "Why not?"

"Did she talk to you about me before the wedding?" He studied her, trying to decide if he could trust her.

"I didn't even know about you until after you were already married. She did send me a picture. Two actually."

"But did you communicate? Did you talk on the phone or whatever it is you guys did?" The question burning through him shouldn't matter. He wanted to know if she'd cared about him at all. Would he have been trying to build a life with someone who was callous? Or had there been something real between them? It might not have been that all-consuming something he thought he'd have with the woman he loved. He'd convinced himself that he could build a future with Autumn and their child.

"Nope, just the wedding pictures. I asked her if I could meet you and I never got a response. Whatever was going on with her back then was obviously big. It wasn't like her to go dark for too long. Although, to be perfectly honest, my sister could be unpredictable."

A shocked cough came out before he could stop it.

"Did she mention the baby?"

Now it was Summer's turn to be floored. Her violet eyes were huge and again her jaw seemed like it was about to hit the floor. "Are you saying what I think you are?"

"That your sister was pregnant? Yes. At least that's what she told me." Everything she'd told him was suspect now. Their entire relationship was tarnished with the latest information he was receiving.

"I'm so sorry." There was so much compassion in those eyes. "Did you ask for verification, like from a doctor?"

"She showed me a positive result on one of those stick tests. I didn't question much after that," he admitted.

"I'm sorry to tell you this." She glanced around like she was searching for the right words. The knot tightening in his gut that told him this was about to get a whole lot worse. "That would have been impossible. We were in a car crash with one of our fosters and my sister took an impact to her midsection. We were in the hospital for weeks. I got these scars." She rolled up her sleeve and showed him a four-inch scar running up her left arm. "My sister injured her abdomen. She had emergency surgery and the doctors had to remove most of her female parts including her fallopian tubes. There's no way my sister was pregnant."

The baby bombshell had been the reason Dawson had asked her to marry him. Looking back, he'd been a fool and he sure as hell felt like it right now. He'd been played in one of the worst possible ways. He muttered a few choice words under his breath, unable to suppress his frustration.

In his line of work, he spent the bulk of his time locking up people who lied, cheated and manipulated. How could he not have realized he was living with one of them?

The answer came quick. She'd been the best. He hadn't seen her deceptions coming. Most criminals were locked up because they weren't smart enough to pull off their crimes. Autumn had been intelligent and, if he was being honest, wounded. She'd brought out all his protective instincts by making him feel like she was alone in the world. He'd let his primal instincts take over, pushing logic out of the way in the process.

When he really thought about it, he deserved everything he was getting.

But, damn, he had to be suspicious of everyone he came across in his line of work. One of his favorite things about living in Katy Gulch and still being connected to his family's ranch was that he could leave work behind him and live a normal life.

In Katy Gulch, he let his guard down. He *could* let his guard down. Almost everyone in town knew each other. There were a few outliers who lived outside town and were very private about their business. They'd learned recently that a woman thought to be a little old lady turned out to be connected to an illegal baby adoption ring. Mrs. Hubert's case had brought up all kinds of questions about his sister's kidnapping decades ago.

Now he felt like he'd been duped in the place where he felt the most relaxed and himself.

"How long did you know my sister before the two of you got married?"

"Clearly not long enough."

Chapter Five

"I'm so sorry," Summer started but was stopped with a warning look from Dawson.

"You already apologized," he pointed out.

"Yes, but I—"

"Feel responsible?" he asked.

She nodded.

"Why? Did you know your sister lied about a pregnancy to get me to marry her?" His question came out more like he'd issued a challenge.

"No." Summer's heart sank. She shouldn't feel responsible for her sister's actions. "It doesn't make me hurt any less for what she put you through."

It was hard to look into his eyes with the admission, but she did anyway. He needed to know how badly she felt.

"I hate to break this news to you, but your sister is a grown woman capable of manipulating grown men. I'm not trying to brag but I'm good at my job. The fact that I lived with a con artist shows how good she was." He didn't add the fact she'd lied to a member of law enforcement and gotten away with it. Or that he must feel so burned right now even though the fact was written all over his face. "If you didn't know or weren't involved, it's not your fault."

Summer issued a sharp sigh. "How could I have not known how much trouble my sister was in?"

"I lived with her and didn't know. If what you're saying is true, and I believe it is, then she disappeared—" He put his hand up to stop her protest. "She tricked me into believing we were going to have a baby *and* a real marriage. Although, I was fool enough to volunteer for that last part to the point she had me thinking getting married because of a child was my idea."

No matter how hard or frustrating this had to be for Dawson, to his credit, he didn't raise his voice. Summer still flinched if there was conflict and especially the sound of a man yelling. Chin out, she could handle whatever came her way but those were hard-won skills.

Whatever had happened to the marriage was one thing, at least he'd cared about her sister.

"I have a lifelong habit of feeling responsible for my sister's actions. I can promise to try to do better and that's as far as I can go right now."

"That's all anyone can ask." He stopped as her stomach reminded both of them she hadn't eaten in a while. His gaze dropped to her midsection. "How about we grab some food and start searching for answers?"

"You'd still help me?" She couldn't hide her shock.

"I have a few days owed to me at work and no big

cases pending. It won't hurt to request time off. Besides, there's a private family matter that has been needing my attention. Maybe we can kill two birds with one stone." He seemed to regret his word choice when he shot a look of apology.

She shook her head. He didn't mean to dredge up bad feelings and he didn't seem convinced that Autumn was gone anyway. With his help, she could get to the bottom of things quicker. If it was any other person besides Dawson O'Connor, she would have doubts about taking his help. The man was a US marshal. He knew how to protect himself. Heck, the ranch had its own security if it wasn't enough that he worked in law enforcement.

"I probably have some leftovers in the fridge if you're not opposed—"

"Anything sounds fine as long as it's not too spicy. I don't do hot." She looked at him and her face flushed.

A ghost of a smile crossed his lips. "How does meatloaf sound?"

"I haven't had meatloaf in… I can't remember how long." Getting help breaking down the details of her sister's case gave Summer the first burst of hope in weeks.

"Meatloaf it is." He pulled out a container and dished food onto two plates. After pushing a couple of buttons on the microwave, the smell filled the kitchen.

"Can I help with anything?" she asked, not used to letting someone else wait on her.

"I'm almost done." He moved to the cabinet and located two glasses. The cotton of his shirt stretched and released over a strong back. Summer diverted her eyes. She had no business ogling Dawson O'Connor's backside.

Looking down at her hand, she realized she was gripping the necklace so tightly there were deep indentations in her left palm. She loosened her grip on the necklace and placed it on top of the small box of her sister's possessions.

"Water okay?" he asked.

"Perfect."

"I figure we can have coffee after we eat while you tell me what you know up to this point and we move on from there."

More of that dangerous hope blossomed. Summer wasn't kidding herself that her sister was out there somewhere still alive despite the fact her heart wanted it to be true. Scrappy and Thick Guy had made it abundantly clear about that. They seemed to have firsthand knowledge that Autumn was gone. It had been a long couple of weeks and more than anything else, she needed answers. Justice had been too much to hope for. Now? There was hope.

Since she'd learned early in life just how slippery a slope hope could be, she wouldn't get too comfortable.

Dawson set a plate down in front of her along with silverware and a glass of water. It was foreign allowing someone to do something for her. Even something so simple as serving food had been off-limits with anyone else.

Summer tried to convince herself that she was too tired to protest. A tiny voice in the back of her mind called her out. There was something easygoing and honest about Dawson that made her relax a little bit around him.

The food was beyond amazing. Before she knew it, she'd cleared her plate. "Did you make this?"

That ghost of a smile returned to his lips—lips she had no business staring at. She refocused.

"Not me. I'm not the best in the kitchen. Laurel cooks up a few meals so it's easy for me to heat something up after work. Other times, I eat at the main house with whoever shows," he said.

Summer wanted to know more about Dawson. She tried to convince herself it had to do with understanding the man who'd made her sister happy, even if it had been for the briefest amount of time.

Again, that voice called her out. She was curious about him for selfish reasons. Reasons she couldn't allow herself to go into now or ever.

"Does your family own this whole ranch?" she asked.

"We're fourth generation cattle ranchers," he said with a nod. She could've sworn his chest expanded with what looked a lot like pride. He finished the last bite of food and took a drink of water. He'd said those words like they were common knowledge. Maybe growing up here in Katy Gulch, it was. She was an outsider despite Dawson making her feel right at home.

It was easy to see why Autumn had fallen for him.

"A dynasty?" The question was meant to be a joke. One look at him stopped her from laughing.

"Something like that." He was serious.

"Okay, what does that even mean?"

"That we're comfortable." So basically, rich.

"Can I ask a question?" Trying to word this without being offensive proved tricky.

"Yeah." It didn't help matters that even when he spoke one word his masculine voice traveled all over her.

"If you own all this land and your family has all this money…why become a US marshal?" Her question caused a low rumble of laughter to escape his serious mouth.

"You said it."

She cocked her head to the side and her eyebrows pinched together.

"My family is wealthy. That gives me a roof over my head that I don't have to pay for and privileges that make life a whole lot easier, like Laurel. But it stops there. I may inherit money, but I have my own life. I live off my own paycheck and invest the money I would've spent on a mortgage. I know how fortunate I am, and I don't take it for granted. If my parents never left me a dime, I'd do just fine on my own. Better than fine."

"Your attitude is impressive. Most people would just ride their legacy out." Summer had even more respect for Dawson now. Even though she'd barely met him didn't mean she didn't know him. He was one of the most down-to-earth people she'd ever met, despite growing up with all this and standing to inherit what must be one of the biggest fortunes in Texas.

He had honor beyond any man she'd ever known. The fact that he would bother to drive to Austin to bail out a woman who'd coldly left him, and to return a box of her prized possessions, struck her heart. He was showing incredible kindness to Summer, despite everything he'd been through. He was concerned about her having a decent meal when he could just try to pin her for answers—answers he deserved.

"Yeah? Seems like a waste of a life to me," he said, like his outlook toward life was no big deal.

"How many siblings do you have?" Getting to know him wasn't helping with her attraction.

"There are seven of us in total but my only sister was kidnapped when she was six months old. She was the firstborn and I doubt Mom would've survived the ordeal if she hadn't found out she was pregnant with my oldest brother a few weeks after."

Summer was stunned. "I can't even imagine what that would do to a mother, let alone being new parents." She studied him. He hadn't even been born at the time of the kidnapping and yet she picked up on something in his voice—a palpable sadness—when he mentioned his sister. "What happened? Did they find her?"

"The case was never solved." He shook his head

before picking up the plates. "My father recently died."

"I'm so sorry." She stopped him with her hand on his arm. The sheer amount of electricity that pulsed through her fingertips startled her. She pulled her hand back and flexed her fingers.

She cleared her throat that had suddenly gone dry. "I can do those."

"Don't worry about it." His voice was trying to come off as casual but there was enough tension for her to realize he'd had the same reaction to physical contact.

"At least let me help."

He stopped for a second and the left corner of his mouth curled. She wondered if he even realized he'd done it. "How about this…you rinse these off and I'll make coffee?"

"Deal." It would give her something to do besides feel like she was betraying her sister with the strong attraction she felt toward Dawson.

Dishes done, fresh coffee in hand, Dawson motioned toward the sofa as she bit back a yawn. She caught him staring at her on the walk over, so he seemed to think it was a good idea to speak his mind when he asked, "When was the last time you slept?"

"It's been a couple of days." She suppressed another yawn. Now that she had a full belly, her body craved rest. Or, maybe it was being around Dawson that allowed her to let her guard down enough to think about dozing off. She'd been sleeping in thirty-minute intervals since arriving in Austin seven days ago.

Seven was the number of days it apparently took to show up in enough places to attract the interest of who she suspected were her sister's killers.

"Think you can sleep now?" He watched as she tried to bite back another yawn.

She took a sip of coffee. "This should help. I want to work on figuring out what happened to Autumn."

"First things first, I need to clear time off with my boss. I'll still have access to law enforcement resources and my guess is we'll need all the help we can get."

Summer didn't feel alone for the first time since this whole ordeal started. And maybe the first time in her whole life, but she didn't want to try to analyze that sentiment now. She sat up straighter and took another sip of coffee. The sofa was made to sink into. She blinked her eyes a couple of times. They'd gone dry on her.

"What do you need me to do?"

There was a laptop on the coffee table that he grabbed and then balanced on his thighs. "You believe your sister was murdered."

He was restating the obvious. "Yes."

"But you don't have proof?"

"No." Again, this was obvious. She wondered where he was going with all this.

"So, I'm looking for a Jane Doe in Austin."

Hearing those words were a hit to Summer's heart. It took a minute for her to be able to respond. "Yes."

A Jane Doe meant an unidentified body.

"She could be in a hospital somewhere." He seemed to be able to read her thoughts. Then again, he was a seasoned investigator. "She would be tagged as Jane Doe if she refused to give her name."

"Hospitals are a good place to start." Summer didn't have it inside her to hope after what the two men chasing her had said.

"And morgues." He was staring at the laptop screen when he seemed to realize how hearing that word might affect Summer. He glanced up and locked eyes. "I'm sorry. I've learned to distance myself from investigations. It's how we get through the rough ones. It doesn't mean that I don't care what happened to Autumn."

"That makes a lot of sense to me actually." Hadn't Summer been doing that on some level for most of her life? Tucking away her emotions. Forcing them somewhere down so deep she couldn't feel anymore. She and Dawson weren't so different.

"It can come off as uncaring but it's really all about focusing every ounce of energy and brain power on finding out the truth."

"And then what?"

"The really bad cases cause you to spend a lot of time at the gym trying to work off the frustration," he said honestly. It also explained why he was in amazing shape.

"Does your work cause you to have a lot of intense days?"

"Yeah," he said with another half smile. "It does.

But there's a pretty big payoff when you take a criminal off the streets and give justice to a family that has been waiting. Everyone deserves that."

She thought about his sister and the fact that her case was never solved. It occurred to her that he brought justice to families when he'd never gotten it for himself or his family.

If she had to guess, he was in his early thirties, which meant the case was several decades old. That was a long time to go without knowing what had happened to a loved one. Her sister's lies to him about a pregnancy when he was the kind of person who wouldn't take that lightly made her angry.

"I'm sorry about your sister, Dawson."

"Thank you." He paused long enough to look at her, catching her gaze and holding on to it. "Now, let's find out what happened to yours."

Chapter Six

Dawson checked the last on his list of hospitals and came up empty. He and Summer had divided the names, working side by side and making call after call. In all, there'd been four Jane Does admitted in the last week to three major hospitals in Austin.

Patient privacy made it tricky to get information but Dawson had a few tricks up his sleeve. He was able to rule out all four Janes, which didn't mean Autumn wasn't in a bed somewhere under a false name.

So, that was a dead-end trail.

The morgue was easier to navigate. There'd been nine Jane Does this month, none of whom fit Autumn's description. If she was dead, her body hadn't shown up anywhere in Austin. There were plenty of places to dump a body in and around Austin. He gave his contact information to the coroner in the event a body showed up that might be a hit.

By eight o'clock, he'd filed a missing persons report and made sure she'd been entered into the database.

It was obvious to him that Summer was running

on fumes, but she refused to go to bed. So, when he saw her slumped over on the couch with her eyes closed, he put a blanket over her and dimmed the lights.

Getting into the groove of treating this like any normal investigation helped. He had a rhythm that went along with ticking boxes off a checklist. Routine was good in times like these.

When he'd made every call on Autumn's behalf that he could, he decided to do a little digging into her personal life. For instance, their marriage.

They'd had a small ceremony. She'd insisted on getting married in Austin and he was beginning to see that the city held a special place in her heart. Especially if that's where she went after she left him. He probably could've traced her, considering they were still legally married for a time. He'd been too busy licking his wounds.

But, now that he thought about it, a few of her actions seemed suspect. Like how she'd insisted on being the one to arrange everything. She'd said that she wanted to be married before they told his family about the pregnancy, insisting that it would lead to less embarrassment in the long run.

He hadn't cared one way or the other. He'd been busy with work and the ranch. So, he'd let her take the lead. She'd also insisted the wedding be just the two of them and Laurel. Again, he'd thought it was a little odd at the time but the most important thing to him had been to become a family so they could get ready for their baby.

The loss Dawson felt when she'd told him she'd lost the baby not long after the wedding still felt real. It had hollowed him out in unexpected ways. For one, he'd known that he wasn't ready to become a father, or a husband for that matter. He was still far too married to his work and kept way too busy on the ranch.

So, the devastation he'd felt when he'd learned about the miscarriage had caught him off guard. Don't get him wrong, he'd been scared as hell after first learning Autumn was pregnant. But he figured no person was ever truly ready for such a life-changing event.

And from firsthand experience he could tell anyone who asked that no one was ever truly ready for the loss, either. Looking back, Autumn had sure played the part. She'd seemed so broken after the news that he felt the need to protect her even more.

The fact she'd played him both ways still stung.

Dawson pulled up the copy of the divorce papers figuring he needed to interview anyone and everyone connected to Autumn. It had been so early in the pregnancy he hadn't been to a doctor's appointment yet. She'd said she had someone she trusted in Austin and had taken several daylong trips to tie up loose ends.

Katy Gulch had an incredible doctor that Dawson's mother had recommended. Autumn had burst into tears at the suggestion of changing doctors. At the time, Dawson's mother reassured him that pregnant women had all kinds of hormones and told him not to take it too personally.

Now he wished he'd asked for the name of her doctor in Austin. Of course, the pregnancy was a sham so she most likely would've made something up. He couldn't exactly count on anything she'd told him.

Which also made him wonder about the friend of hers, supposedly a minister who she'd insisted marry them. Dawson had asked for the marriage certificate so he could add her to his work benefits and she'd stalled big-time.

Had she backed herself into a corner?

The obvious reason someone would want to pin him down for marriage was money. But she hadn't asked for or taken a dime. Looking back, it was also the reason he'd signed the divorce papers so easily. She'd wanted nothing but her freedom. He'd been too hurt and angry to fight back. His pride had been wounded. He'd scribbled his name on the dotted line after reviewing the document and then mailed it back after making a copy for his records.

He wouldn't make the mistake of not fact-checking another relationship.

There'd been no need to cancel her insurance at work because he'd never officially added her to anything. Considering he'd never been married before, he took her word for everything. Why wouldn't he? She was his wife. Adding her to his insurance was a simple thing to him. She'd said something about being covered under a different policy that didn't run out until the end of the year.

In his personal life, he'd never been betrayed. Had that made him naive?

Dawson pulled up his divorce file and searched for the name of her attorney. Matt Charley Shank. There was no address on the letterhead, which was odd. He found it in the body of the second page.

Dawson typed in the name to get a phone number. He shouldn't be surprised at the search results. There was no Matt Charley Shank listed as an attorney in Austin.

He flexed and released his fingers a couple of times to work out some of the tension. He needed to hit the gym for a good workout but there was no time. He could, however, fire off a few push-ups. He had a set of weights in the garage for those times when he needed a quick workout.

This seemed like one of those times. But first, he checked the internet for the name of Autumn's minister friend, Grover Hart, to see what church he belonged to. Not a huge surprise at this point when Dawson learned Grover Hart's services could be bought and paid for. His big claim to fame? Weddings, no licenses required.

If the attorney was a sham and the minister was a sham, the marriage had to be a sham.

SUMMER STOOD IN the opened doorway leading into the garage. A heavy metal band played low in the background. It was the middle of the night. A shirtless Dawson pumped weights. Her gaze lingered a little too long on his muscled chest, mesmerized by the tiny beads of sweat.

She forced her gaze away and cleared her dry throat.

"Sorry to interrupt, is it okay if I use the restroom to freshen up?" she asked.

He didn't seem surprised that she'd been standing there and that made her cheeks burn with embarrassment. Getting caught staring at him didn't top her list of things to do when she woke up. She was still trying to figure out how she'd fallen asleep in the first place.

She'd woken to a dimly lit room with a blanket placed over her.

"Make yourself at home." He sat up and grabbed a towel.

Summer forced herself to look away as he toweled off his face. He stood up. He still had on jeans that hung low on lean hips. He had the kind of body she'd expect to see on a billboard somewhere. His abs were cut. His arms strong. His waist lean. Don't even get her started on how gorgeous he was.

Dawson O'Connor was the total package. Intelligent. Decent. Smokin' hot. And fierce. He had a look in his eyes that said he wouldn't hesitate to go all in to protect someone he cared about. He also had the kind of confidence that said he could back it up, too.

An attraction to her sister's ex-husband couldn't happen. The electricity she felt radiating from him was most likely residual desire that he felt for Autumn, not Summer. He had, in fact, loved her sister enough to marry her. Granted, Autumn had played a dirty trick to get him to ask. But his feelings for her sister must run deep.

"I can show you where everything is." He tossed the towel onto the weight bench and headed in her direction. She immediately took a few steps back to allow him room to pass by. She needed to put as much distance between them as humanly possible.

Dawson paused long enough to make eye contact as he walked by. There was something in his eyes she couldn't quite put her finger on. Was looking at her in the home they were supposed to share like seeing a ghost?

"I'm sorry. I must remind you of her," she said softly.

"You'd think that would be the case but I couldn't help noticing how different you both are. Beautiful without a doubt, but now that I've had a chance to get to know you, I was just thinking how different you look to me. Strange how personality affects looks once the initial impression wears off. You know?"

"Yeah." She did know. She couldn't count the number of times she met an attractive man only to get to know him and never see him in the same light again. That wasn't the case with Dawson. His personality enhanced already drop-dead gorgeous looks. The saying that beauty was only skin deep came to mind. It was so true. There was so much more to a person and she'd been turned off countless times by outwardly attractive, inwardly awful people.

Summer followed Dawson to the opposite side of

the main living area and down a hallway. There were several opened doors revealing an office, a bedroom and a bathroom.

"This is the guest suite. Make yourself comfortable."

She had little more than the clothes on her back and her handbag. He looked her over and moved to the closet.

"Laurel's niece is probably about your size. Rachel is a grad student in Houston and has stayed here a few times. She left behind a jogging suit if you want to borrow it."

"Thanks. I'll take you up on that offer," she said.

"I can throw your clothes in the wash while you shower if you want." The thought of Dawson handling her undergarments had her shaking her head. That was a hard no. She didn't want the image of him touching any of her personal belongings anywhere in her thoughts. Fighting the attraction when he stood this close was difficult enough. She didn't need to add mental images to the equation.

"I'll take care of it when I'm out of the shower if you point me in the direction," she quickly said. Too quickly.

He studied her for a long moment before he spoke again.

"I didn't find a Jane Doe in any of the hospitals I called or at the morgue."

"Any hits on the missing persons report or is it too early?" she asked.

"Never too early to hope but no."

"I can draw them out again if—"

"Hell, no. I won't risk your safety."

"It might be the fastest way to find out who we're dealing with," she countered.

"I won't argue your point and it's easy to see that you care about your sister. Let me do this the right way and investigate in a way that keeps you safe in the process. Okay with you?" Those intense penetrating eyes swayed her away from running off half-cocked. Doing that so far had almost gotten her killed. She reminded herself that she wasn't alone in this. Dawson had resources she didn't. Plus, she couldn't bring justice for her sister if Summer was dead.

She took in a deep breath. "Okay."

"I'll let you know if anything comes in while you grab a shower."

Thanking Dawson didn't seem nearly enough to cover her gratitude. It was a starting point.

He nodded before stepping into the hallway. With his hand on the door, he said, "You have this whole wing to yourself. Do you want the door open or closed?"

"I'll close it." She did before getting her bearings in the oversize guest room. One door led to a walk-in closet and another led to a large bathroom. There were fresh towels hanging and, she noticed, a white bathrobe on the back of the door.

There were shampoos on hand as well as fresh toothbrushes and toothpaste. The place was stocked and ready for company. Mostly likely Laurel's doing.

Summer doubted someone who kept a full-time job as a marshal while still working the family ranch had time to think about stocking a guest bath.

She was grateful for Laurel. Now that she really thought about it, she'd like to circle back to the woman and have a conversation. If she and Autumn used to talk, maybe there was some hint there as to what Autumn's life had been like.

Again, guilt struck that Summer hadn't been more in tune with her sister. To be fair, Autumn was complicated. She marched to her own drum and had a tendency to go all-in before going all-out. She could be charming. And, although she and Summer shared the same genes, Autumn knew how to make the most of their looks.

To Summer's thinking, her sister had always been the prettier one of the two despite starting from the same blank canvas.

She showered in record time, thinking how great a cup of coffee would taste about now. She'd only managed a few sips of the other one before she'd conked out on the sofa. Like everything at Katy Bull Ranch, the coffee tasted better than anywhere else.

Autumn had found a sanctuary here. Why would she ever leave?

Had she gotten bored of the ranch? Best as she could remember about the timeline, Autumn and Dawson had only been together a few months before she'd played the pregnancy card. Summer was still mortified and embarrassed on her sister's behalf for that one.

And then what? How long had they been together before her sister had broken the news to him there was no baby? The web of lies was going to take some time and some untangling to find the truth. An honest man like Dawson would be frustrated by her sister's antics. Someone else might not handle the situation the same. Which begged the question, *was there someone else?*

Summer needed to sit down and develop a timeline. She always did her best thinking when she could see everything written on paper.

After meeting Dawson, even more questions simmered. One bubbled to the surface. Had Autumn come to Katy Gulch to hide and then found protection in Dawson O'Connor too good to pass up?

Chapter Seven

"Coffee smells amazing." Even the sound of Summer's voice was different from her sister's. He couldn't believe he'd ever thought she was his ex. And she looked even more beautiful after a few hours of sleep.

"I waited for you to get out of the bathroom to pour a cup." Dawson turned toward the voice and his chest tightened when he saw Summer standing at the kitchen doorway wearing the sweat suit on loan from Rachel. She had wadded up her clothes into a ball that she held.

There shouldn't be anything sexy about the clothes she had on. The material was standard cotton, and the top was tight at the waist. She had the zipper gripped so tight with her free hand there was no way the thing was moving.

He chalked up his reaction to her to simple biology. She was a beautiful woman, even more so as he got to know her. There was enough electricity pinging between them to light an entire house anytime the two stood close to each other.

Even at this distance, his body heated. And it was more than physical attraction. His heart fisted and he was in trouble. Then again, after the case was solved, she'd go back to living her life and he'd go back to his.

"Washer and dryer are down the other hallway." He was pretty damn certain there was no annual Christmas card obligation to his ex-wife's sister. He hadn't even known about her until she'd dropped the bomb on him that she was Autumn's sister. He'd shot off an email to one of his buddies to verify what he already knew in his heart, she was being honest about her identity.

His need to verify every new person in his life sat hard on his chest. He was used to being suspicious in his job but had always surrounded himself with good people. With Autumn, he'd had a lapse in judgment.

Something else had been gnawing at the back of his mind. A pathological liar believed their own lies. It was what made them so good at delivering them. The fact that she was a pathological liar made him think twice about what he'd discovered from the internet last night as he poured a cup of coffee for Summer and tried to shake the fresh-from-the-shower image out of his thoughts.

Work started on a ranch at 4 a.m. sharp so waking up at this time wasn't uncommon. To a normal person, this was the middle of the night and Grover Hart would fall under the category of "normal" person when it came to sleep patterns. That was as much leeway as Dawson would give the man.

Again, Dawson was kicking himself for letting his guard down with the wrong person. Those mistakes felt the worst. Trusting someone when he should've known better made him kick himself twice as hard.

By the time Summer returned, he'd gotten hold of his frustration enough to hand over the mug he'd filled. Fresh-faced, her skin practically glowed. Thick, black lashes hooded violet eyes he could stare into for days.

She took a sip and he cleared his dry throat.

"Can you eat something?" he asked, trying to deflect much of his out-of-control reaction to her. Long, silky hair was still damp from the shower— a shower he didn't want to think much more about for obvious reasons.

"I couldn't eat another bite after filling up on that meatloaf a few hours ago. I'm still full." Her voice was a little too husky, a little too sexy. "It was heaven. Laurel must be a great cook."

Dawson had to fight every instinct he had not to lean in and kiss her. He imagined the horror on her face if he followed through with the impulse and that was a reality slap. Good. He needed to keep a clear mind.

"Did your sister ever mention any names to you in the past year or two?" he asked.

"Besides you? No. And she only gave me your first name in the beginning. I finally matched your picture to a news article." She took a sip of coffee and leaned her hip against the counter.

"How about Matt, Charley or Shank? Do any of

those names sound familiar?" Following along the lines of Autumn being a pathological liar, she would use names that she wouldn't mix up easily. It was part of believing the lies.

Summer closed her eyes like she was reaching back as far as she could into her memory bank. "Seems like there was a Charley at some point."

Dawson retrieved a notepad and pen from the small built-in desk in the kitchen. He set them on top of the granite island and scribbled the names in those variations.

"You like to write stuff down?" she asked.

"Seems like everyone uses computers now. Call me old-fashioned but I like pen and paper," he admitted with a small smile.

"Same here. It's just easier for me to look at something when it's on paper for some crazy reason." She shook her head. "Go figure."

He didn't want to notice the similarities between him and Summer. He didn't want to notice how naturally beautiful she was or how a small line creased her forehead when she really concentrated. Or how sexy it was when it happened. He didn't want to notice how full her pink lips were or how sweet they would probably taste.

Dawson refocused on the piece of paper.

"What is it? Is there something on my face?" she asked.

"Nope. Your face is perfect." He caught his slip a few words too late. They were out there and he couldn't reel them back in now.

"Oh." The one word was all she said. He wished she'd said it with a little more shock or maybe even disgust. Instead, it was surprise and something that sounded a lot like hope.

Dawson's cell buzzed, a welcome break into the moment happening between them. He walked over to the sofa where he'd left it and then checked the screen.

"Hey, what did you find out?" he asked his buddy from work, Anderson Willis. Law enforcement worked round the clock and Anderson was one of the few people Dawson could call at this hour.

"I'm sorry to break the news to you, Dawson," came the familiar voice. "There's no record of you ever being married."

It was a double-edged sword. He shook off the shock and said, "I owe you one for tracking this answer down for me."

"You know I have your back."

"I appreciate it." Dawson ended the call and then looked to Summer. "Turns out, the wedding was a fake. I was never married to your sister."

"Why would she go through all that?" she asked.

"It explains a lot actually. She only wanted the two of us there for the ceremony with Laurel as a witness. Autumn insisted on handling all the details herself. I learned a few hours ago that the man who 'married' us was a for-hire and not a longtime family friend."

"But why trap you into marriage with a fake pregnancy story only to find out there'd never been a wedding in the first place?"

If he knew the answer to that question, he'd be so far ahead of the game. Investigations were like puzzles. Evidence often came one or a few pieces at a time. Sometimes the motive didn't make sense until all the pieces were in place.

This would most likely be one of those complicated cases.

"We'll start with the name Charley. It isn't much to go on but we'll know to pay special attention if his name comes up."

She moved over to the notepad, picked up the pen, wrote down the name.

"There was a coffee shop on Capital Avenue where my sister used to go. One of the workers did a double take when I showed up and it made me think he knew her. It could just be that she got coffee there when she was in town but the way he looked at me with…*surprise*… I guess is the right word…made me think there was something more to it."

"Capital Coffee?"

She nodded.

"I know that place," he said, trying to think of any politicians he knew with the first name of Charley. A political tie could explain her murder if she'd rubbed a politician the wrong way or if this was someone from her past. Austin was the capital. If she hung out at a coffee shop that was a known hangout for politicians, it could give them a direction.

"We need to look up any politician with the name

Charley." That wouldn't be too difficult. Their names were public record.

"Or a political aid." She was right. And it made the list a whole lot longer and harder to track down.

"The only other people who frequent that coffee shop are UT professors. I doubt she'd have a run-in with one of those." Ideas started churning and they were making progress. Inching along at this point but he'd take what he could get. "How'd you find out about the coffee shop?"

"She sent me a picture from there a couple of times."

"It's a starting point. I don't like the idea of taking you back to Austin, though. Not while this situation is hot." He didn't doubt his skills in protecting a witness. One of the most important rules of the program was that the witness not return to the town from which they were relocated.

Technically, she wasn't the one being tracked. The men chasing her didn't seem to know that. If Autumn had hid her twin sister from her so-called husband, she probably didn't talk about her family member with any of the men she'd dated.

That might mean no one would ever go looking for Summer. She could be safe if she went back to her life in Washington. Even though he highly doubted she'd go for what he was about to pitch, he had to do it anyway.

"What do you think of letting me take over the investigation from here?" He'd barely finished his sentence before she started shaking her head.

"No way." The finality in those words told him not to argue.

"Would you at least think about stepping back?"

The look she shot him made words unnecessary.

"The only reason I bring it up is because I can protect you better if you go back to your normal life and let me lead the investigation into your sister's case." He had a moral obligation to make her aware of her options.

She didn't immediately respond. Her lips were set in a thin line. She'd made up her mind. Instead of overreacting, she seemed to take a minute to pick apart his reasoning. The small crease appeared on her forehead. "I think I understand what you really mean. I understand the risks I'm taking. Believe me. I barely got away and I know that was sheer dumb luck. I got even luckier that, despite what my sister did to you, you are a decent enough human being to actually want to help. So, I'm not taking it for granted."

He was impressed with how well she'd thought out her response.

"You have a big family, right?"

"Yes," he confirmed.

"You guys are all close based on what you've told me so far." Her argument was already being laid out for her the minute she brought his family into it.

"That's right."

"My sister is all I have in the world. She might not be perfect. Believe me when I say that I can count the ways in which she isn't. But we made a pact to have each other's backs. I told her that I'd always be there for her. I've let her down in the worst possible way. There's so much that I'd do differently now. I can't go back. I can't change what has happened. I can't bring her back. All I can do is nail the bastards who hurt her."

There were only two words appropriate as a response. "Fair enough."

THE WASHING MACHINE BUZZED. Summer forced her shoulders to relax. "I know where to go."

The washing machine was down the same hallway as the garage. The hallway was longer and there was a window at the end. She moved her clothes through to the dryer, pushing the sexy sweaty images of Dawson out of her thoughts. It was probably good that she would only know Dawson for a few more days before heading back to Washington and to her life there.

Not that she had much of one. She'd been saving tips to take a few computer classes so she could get a nine-to-five job. She wasn't particular about where she worked as long as it didn't involve hustling drinks or food. She'd done both. Often at the same time to make rent.

Summer and her sister had had a crazy dream when they were little of owning their own shop. When they were super little, the dream had been to open a toy store and then they'd wanted a small bookstore. At least, Summer had. Autumn had said she didn't care as long as there was a coffee shop attached for her to manage.

Then, her sister started drifting around and moved farther and farther away, not just physical distance. The calls had stopped coming. Autumn was later and later returning Summer's calls.

The reason Summer had been working in restaurants and bars was to save up enough to start their business. She'd been working every job from waitress to assistant manager trying to learn everything she could about running a business.

Everything came to an abrupt stop after Autumn sent news she got married. Her life was going to be with her husband and she said that Summer shouldn't worry about finances because Autumn had married well.

At first, Summer questioned whether or not her sister had married for a bank account. The look on her face in the wedding picture had given Summer hope that wasn't the case. Finding out her sister had forced Dawson's hand still didn't sit well. Now there was the fact she'd actually never truly been married in the first place.

But she'd wanted Summer to believe she was married, and still was married. She turned on the dryer and headed back to the kitchen. She walked over to the pen and wrote down the word *married*.

"My sister didn't tell me about the divorce." She flashed eyes at him. "Even though it was all fairy tale or smoke and mirrors, however you look at it."

"It wasn't real," he seemed quick to confirm.

"But she wanted me to believe it. I'm wondering if she wanted someone else to believe it, too."

"Possibly someone named Charley?" he asked.

"It's all I can think of," she said. "It worked with me. I really thought she was happy and I stopped worrying about her." The fact she'd rarely returned messages in the past year had barely registered with Summer. "I was busy coming up with a Plan B for my life after hers seemed settled."

"So, her wanting you to believe she was married was important," he agreed.

"It's also strange that she left this box here." She motioned toward the wooden box with what was supposed to be her sister's most prized possessions. "She knew she was leaving. Right?"

"I believe so."

"Then, why take off without something so personal? I'm guessing the way she left things with you that she never intended to come back," she said.

He rocked his head. "That's been my assumption this whole time. The main reason someone leaves something of value behind is the person is in such a rush they forget it."

"I'm probably just wanting to see the best in my sister but I wonder if she left my necklace because she wanted to protect my identity." She picked up the pendant and let it rest on her flat palm.

"It's highly possible." He reached for the pen she'd set down and wrote "protect loved one."

"Have you considered that she might have been trying to protect you?" she asked him.

"It crossed my mind that she picked me for my ability to protect *her*." His response was honest, and she could give him that. There was far more hurt in his tone when he talked about Autumn now. He'd said before that he was in full-on investigator mode.

"That might be true. She seemed like she was hiding and making rash decisions. Some of it feels illogical."

"We have a lot of puzzle pieces missing," he agreed before glancing at the wall clock. "In a couple of hours, we leave for Austin."

His cell buzzed and this time it was still sitting on the granite island. He walked over to it. The look on his face when he checked the screen nearly stopped her heart.

Chapter Eight

"Thank you for letting me know."

Those six words were going to change Summer's life forever. She just knew it. Her legs gave and she smacked her hand on the island to stop herself from going down. All along, she'd known it. And yet confirmation of her sister's death nearly pulled her under.

Dawson was by her side in the next second, his strong hand steadying her, helping her stay upright.

"I'm sorry." Two words she hated more than anything in that moment.

He helped her to the couch and brought a fresh cup of coffee. For a long time, she couldn't speak as tears streamed. Dawson gave her space. He set his laptop up at the granite countertop and took a stool. He'd moved it to the side presumably so he could keep an eye on her.

Summer didn't want to know the details of what had happened just yet. She just sat there, suspended in time, unable to think or speak. Her brain refused to process. A fog descended, cloaking her with a heaviness that pressed so hard on her chest she could barely breathe.

Sipping coffee to try to jar herself out of the haze of grief, she hugged a pillow to her chest.

The dryer went off at some point. She didn't care. She heard Dawson move around without really registering what he was doing. The coffee in her cup had long since gone cold. She rolled the mug around in her palms.

Tears dried up at some point. She couldn't be certain when and didn't care. The sun came up and she cursed the fact. How could life go on when her heart had just been ripped out of her chest?

Come on, she finally tried to rally. She'd known this news was coming. She'd had time to deal with it. There was something extra devastating about that final blow, something extra cruel and final. She curled up on her side and pulled the blanket from last night over herself, suddenly feeling very cold.

The details could wait. In a few hours, she'd learn the condition of what would now be referred to as *the body*. She hoped like hell there was some evidence, a fingerprint or piece of DNA that could bring closure to the case and justice for her sister.

A small part of her didn't want this investigation to end. She didn't want to go back to the nonlife she'd had in Washington. The one where she had no real purpose anymore.

But then if wishes were being granted, she wanted her sister back. No matter how irresponsible Autumn had been or how lost, there had been something very good inside her that had been worth fighting for. At least Summer thought so.

Summer leaned forward and set the mug on the coffee table. A few seconds later, Dawson brought over a plate of food. She glanced at it, figuring there was no way that a breakfast sandwich was going down. It could go down but she highly doubted it would stay there for long.

The glass of water, on the other hand, she decided to try.

"Okay if I sit with you?" Dawson asked.

"I'd like that a lot." She meant it, too. The only light in this dark situation was the fact she hadn't been alone when she'd heard the news. Having been on her own for most of her life caused her to learn to depend on herself early. Being completely alone for the rest of her life was one of her worst fears. She'd been so afraid that if she lost her sister she would fade away, too.

She scooted over enough for him to sit next to her. It was unexpected for him to be her comfort. But she didn't hesitate for a second when he tugged her toward him.

Burying her face in his chest, she released the pent-up frustration that had been simmering for years.

DAWSON KNEW BETTER than to be Summer's comfort for too long. It was dangerous territory for him because it would be all too easy to get lost in her violet eyes. He couldn't argue how right she felt in his arms. Instead of giving in to what he wanted, he put up a wall.

His mind was still spinning from everything he'd learned in the past twenty-four hours. Autumn's lies stacked up from the fake pregnancy to the fact she never went to college or had a living relative. There was a lot to unpack and try to digest. Even though a year had passed, learning he'd been lied to and tricked caused all his old walls to shoot up. The thought of letting anyone else in seemed about as appealing as drinking motor oil.

Except, when it came to Summer, he found that he wanted to trust. There was a quiet strength and vulnerability in her that touched him in a deep place. Losing Autumn had hurt his pride. Losing Summer would break his heart.

Dawson's cell buzzed where he'd left it on the granite island. Summer tensed and then pulled back as though she realized the worst blow had already been delivered. It had. He couldn't imagine losing one of his brothers out of the blue like that.

He pushed up to standing and got to his phone in time to answer after a glance at the screen. "Hey, Colton."

His older brother was sheriff but there was no need for formalities.

"I wish I had better news." The fact that Colton was getting right to the point sent an icy chill racing down Dawson's spine.

"What is it?" Dawson asked.

"It's Dad. A private investigator came forward

and said he gave Dad information about possible known associations of Mrs. Hubert a few weeks before Dad's death. Someone might've come onto the property to stop him. And there's more."

"What else?" The question had to be asked.

"Someone used his credit card two days ago, so we're diving in to figure out who and how the person got it." Colton said.

"If Dad was following up on a lead and that's what got him killed, would the killer be crazy enough to use the credit card?" Dawson asked.

"It's a reasonable assumption. The fact that his credit card was used a few days ago could mean a lot of things. He might've dropped his wallet and someone found it before he was murdered."

"True." There was no need for them to go over all the possibilities since both worked in law enforcement and both had seen plenty in their time on the job.

"Where was his credit card used?" Dawson asked.

"Convenience store in Beckridge."

"That's not far. There'd be camera footage. Right?"

"The Mart doesn't keep the recordings. They wipe them out every day. It would be impossible to know who used the credit card based on any footage," Colton explained.

"We could determine if the person was male or female, though. And the clerk might have a description. Let's see, the highway runs straight through there." Dawson was grasping at straws, hoping for a witness.

"The clerk couldn't remember who used the card.

And, I talked to mother and she wanted to increase the size of the reward for information about Dad's murder. What do you think about that?" Colton asked.

"Ten thousand dollars is already a lot of money for someone to do the right thing."

"You won't get any arguments out of me there." At least he and his brother were on the same page.

"Did you tell her that might invite gold diggers into the party? The amount of false leads would go through the roof if we increased it five or ten thousand dollars?" Dawson asked.

"I sure did."

Dawson was preaching to the choir. His brother was a top-notch sheriff and would have already thought of all those things.

"For the record, I'm against the idea. I think it'll bring too many quacks out of the woodwork. You probably have your hands full as it is with a ten-thousand-dollar reward," Dawson said.

"All of us are in unison on that," Colton confirmed. He, no doubt, would have contacted their other siblings.

"Changing subjects. Are you doing okay with *everything*?" Colton asked. The emphasis he'd placed on the last word gave a strong hint that he was talking about Summer.

Dawson wasn't ready to discuss anything about the sisters with his brother just yet. Especially not where he was on a personal level with Summer and he knew that was the real question Colton was asking. Dawson paused for a minute and the pieces started clicking together. Given how many of his brothers worked in law enforcement, the news about Autumn's death would've traveled through the family by now. He'd intended to call his brothers once he got his mind around the news. For now, Summer had been and still was his priority.

"We have a lot going on over here. I'm planning a road trip to Austin in a couple of hours. There are a few people I want to interview over there," he said. "And if we can keep the news about Autumn as quiet as possible, I'd appreciate it. And that goes for everyone who knows, not just the family."

The news about Autumn had been hard but not because of any residual emotions. He'd turned those off a while ago and was down to a bruised ego. Any anger he had toward her dissipated the minute he heard she was in trouble. It explained a lot about the way she'd acted. He was down to being genuinely sorry for her and her family on a human level rather than as an ex-husband. Hell, their marriage had been too brief for him to put down roots in the relationship. She'd swept in and out of his life like a spring thunderstorm.

"It's true. What you heard about Autumn," he said to his brother.

"I saw Laurel yesterday. I was in the barn when she brought Shadow over."

"Then you've probably pieced together the fact that Autumn has an identical twin sister. She's here and I'm going to help her see this through." Dawson braced himself for the argument that was sure to come from his brother—a brother who would have Dawson's best interest at heart without a doubt.

"You know each and every one of us is here if you need *anything*." The way he emphasized that last word suggested the offer covered more than their brotherly bond. There was a hint of confusion in Colton's tone, which was understandable under the circumstances.

Dawson had no way to discuss something he didn't understand for himself. That "something" was his need to make this right for Summer.

"You say you're heading to Austin in a little while?" Colton brought the subject back to the investigation.

"That's right."

"You want any of us to tag along?" Colton asked.

"I got this. I appreciate the offer, though." Dawson figured he had enough contacts in Austin to get backup if anything went down. For now, he wanted to visit a coffee shop and a so-called minister. An internet search of Texas lawmakers didn't reveal anyone with the first name of Charles or Charley.

"You know I'm just a phone call and a couple of hours away if you need anything. I'm also pretty decent with the database, so if you need any help with research, I'm here for that, too," Colton offered.

"I appreciate you more than you know."

"It's what we do for each other. Right?" Colton said. It was true. Any one of them would drop what they were doing on a moment's notice for the other one.

Dawson thanked his brother before ending the call. He moved to the sink and filled a glass with water, and then polished it off. He'd pace if it would do any good. Frustration built when he thought about someone using his father's credit card like it was nothing, like they knew they wouldn't get caught. Finn O'Connor was strong and tough for any age. Under most conditions, he would have been able to hold his own. *Most* being the operative word.

Anyone could be taken down under the right conditions no matter how strong or well prepared. He needed to make a pit stop at the convenience store on the way to Austin. Shadow would be okay hanging out in the barn for a couple of days. He'd have to let the ranch foreman know, but that was easy enough. Shadow loved being at the barn so no reason to feel bad there. Apollo could certainly use the company.

From behind him, he heard the sound of Summer's bare feet on the wood floor. He could sense she was moving toward him. Her clean, fresh-flower smell filled his senses when he took in a breath meant to calm himself.

"Was that news about your father?" Summer's voice traveled over him, detonating in his heart.

"Yes. His credit card is in play a couple of towns over." He heard the hurt in his own voice when he spoke about his father—hurt he was usually so good at masking.

He set the glass down on the counter and released his hold on it for fear he might break it. He gripped the bullnose edge of the granite countertop instead.

There were a whole lot of *should not*s rolling around in Dawson's thoughts. He should not turn around. He should not take a step toward Summer. He sure as hell should not kiss her. But that's exactly what he did.

Dawson dipped his head down and captured those sweet, full, pink lips. He exhaled against her mouth as her tongue darted out.

Now it was Summer's turn to take in a breath as he pressed his lips against hers harder and the two melded together. She pushed up on her tiptoes and brought her hands up, tunneling her fingers in his hair as she took the lead, deepening the kiss.

Electricity pulsed through his body, bringing him back to life. He looped his hands around her waist as she pressed her body flush with his. Through the cotton material of the robe, he could feel her full breasts against his stomach. She was perfection and fit him perfectly.

She parted her lips, which gave him better access, and he drove his tongue inside her mouth. She tasted like dark roast coffee and a little bit of peppermint from brushing her teeth earlier. Dark roast coffee mixed with peppermint was his new favorite flavor.

Dawson's pulse skyrocketed and his heart jackhammered his ribs. Summer molded against him. When she opened her eyes and pulled back just enough for him to see those incredible violet eyes of hers, his heart detonated.

She seemed to search his gaze and he knew what was coming next.

"Is this a good idea, Dawson?" she asked.

Looking into those eyes, he couldn't imagine doing anything with her would be a bad idea. Bad timing? Now that was a thing.

If he'd met her two years ago or a year and a half ago, it would be so much easier to get lost in her. Now timing was a problem. He couldn't go back and undo the past. Normally, he understood the value of life lessons and hard situations. He could appreciate how deep he had to reach and how much he had to grow when times were tough.

Selfishly, he wanted Summer. He wanted those bright violet eyes and sweet lips. He wanted to get lost and forget how complicated all of this was.

Dawson muttered a curse under his breath. Because timing.

"Probably not." It was difficult to say that, considering their kiss brought him to life in places that had been dead too long. No one had caused that kind of reaction from him with something so simple before Summer. Timing.

"Then, we should probably put a stop to this." The uncertainty in her voice made him want to convince her otherwise. It didn't seem like it would take a whole lot and it definitely wouldn't on his part.

Her body pressing against his wasn't making it any easier to think straight. She had the kind of curves that made her feel like a real woman. Long legs, soft round bottom, she was perfect, sexy...

Dawson stopped himself right there. His arms still looped around her waist, he dipped his head down and feathered a kiss on her bottom lip. "I want to do this. I sure as hell don't want to stop. But, the last thing I want to do is confuse the situation any more than we already have."

Those words were a bad idea. He heard how they sounded coming out of his mouth and the hurt in her eyes compounded it. The thing was, he could see himself going *there* with her. He could easily see himself doing the get-to-know-her-better thing. He wanted to know all those little details about her that made up a relationship. Could he?

Could she? Could she stick around long enough to see if there was anything deeper than spark between them? Could she stay in one place long enough to figure out if this could ignite into a flame? See if there was any substance to turn initial attraction into something so much more?

There was nothing inside Dawson that wanted to jump into another serious relationship. He would doubt his own judgment every step of the way because of Autumn. She'd burned him enough to back away from the stove the second time.

An annoying voice in the back of his head told him he was making up excuses. Was he?

Hell, maybe he was the one who needed some distance. Nothing in his body or mind or heart wanted to take a step back from Summer. And that was dangerous under the circumstances.

He could make all the arguments he wanted to. The truth was that while he was standing toe to toe with Summer, he couldn't force himself to be the one to step back. She would have to do it. And she did.

Which also told him she could.

If he was going to guard his heart, he was going to have to do a better job than that.

Turned out Summer Grayson was his weak spot. Dawson needed to get more control over his emotions. The phrase "get a grip" came to mind.

What he needed was to get a handle before this became a runaway train.

The first time he'd seen Summer opened up a sore wound. Although, to be honest, she had seemed different from Autumn from the moment he laid eyes on her. He'd noticed all those quirks that were uniquely hers. Her personality could not be more opposite her sister despite a likeness. And he stopped there at a resemblance.

Dawson couldn't think of Autumn and Summer as identical because they were so different. Summer had that fresh-from-the-shower face. She looked like she ran a brush through her hair and let it flow.

Autumn, on the other hand, spent quite a bit of time in the bathroom tinkering around with her looks. Being around her triggered his protective instincts, but that wasn't the same as love. She'd been helpless and he'd stepped in. To be fair, he'd always seen himself with an independent, spirited wife for the long haul. Someone who could challenge his thinking and yet be silly enough to laugh at herself because life was guaranteed to deliver some hard knocks.

Summer, on the other hand, was strong. Yes, vulnerable, too. There was a certain undeniable vulnerability about her, which wasn't the same as helplessness. Summer was the roll-up-her-sleeves type. If something needed doing, she was going to do it. She was far from a helpless victim.

Her personality couldn't have been more opposite from her sister's. Summer was quick-witted and resourceful. She was beyond intelligent. And, man, did she possess a strength about her, a dignity that he'd rarely ever witnessed.

He had to fight every instinct that had him wanting, no needing, to be as close to her as he physically could. Summer just had that way about her. She was like the sun. He wanted to tilt his face toward it and take in its warmth.

Dawson reminded himself once again that Summer lived in Washington and he lived in Texas. Those were a lot of miles to cover. And that was the easiest part about a relationship between the two of them.

"Where to first?" Again, her voice traveled over him, bringing to life those places that had been dormant far too long.

"I'd like to interview Grover Hart first. See if he knew your sister beyond her locating him on the internet. Maybe he can give us some insight into where she hung out and what she did while she was in Austin."

"It sounds like a good place to start." She paused for a few seconds and he could almost see the wheels spinning in her brain. "Is there some way we could change the way I look? Is there something here like a scarf or maybe a ball cap that I can wear?"

"I'm already a few steps ahead of you on that one. I do have to get witnesses to safety from time to time so I keep a duffel bag full of supplies in the closet. We'll be traveling during the day and it's sunny, so I have a variety of sunglasses for you to choose from. I definitely have scarves and a few other things I think you might find helpful," he said.

Dawson turned toward the front door and motioned to the closet. He also had to force his gaze away from her backside when she headed over to the closet.

Watching her walk away wasn't going to do good things to Dawson. He was still kicking himself for not having a better answer when the two of them had been close. And he probably would be for a very long time if he let her get away.

Chapter Nine

Summer didn't realize she was tapping her finger against the window on the passenger side of Dawson's truck until he glanced over at her. His look was one of concern, not annoyance. She realized her nervous tick was in full swing.

She'd like to say her thoughts were consumed with what they were about to face in interviewing Grover Hart, the internet minister, but that wouldn't exactly be true. Her thoughts kept winding back to the kiss she'd shared with Dawson in the kitchen and the way it held the kind of passion that had been missing in every kiss for her entire life.

Since that was about as productive as squeezing a turnip and expecting blood, she did her best to shove those thoughts aside.

Grover Hart lived far north of Austin in a small town called Bluff. His house sat on what looked like at least an acre of land, and mostly resembled a junkyard. There were tractor parts and what she assumed were truck parts littering the lawn. There was a couch that looked like an '80s relic sitting next to the front porch steps of the small bungalow.

Dawson parked and kept the engine idling. He glanced over at Summer one more time, his gaze lingering a little bit longer this time.

"This should be interesting," he said.

"I couldn't agree more."

On the east side of the house was a small white gazebo. There were fake flowers wound through the slats. She imagined this was a place Grover performed quick ceremonies. Her sister and Dawson had married on his family's ranch. She shuddered, thinking about the kind of person who would be on the outskirts of town needing a quickie wedding in basically a junkyard. She also wondered how legal the nuptials would be. That was a whole different issue altogether.

"Guess we better do this." Dawson shut off the engine and exited the driver's seat. By the time he got around to the passenger side, she'd let herself out. There was a small look of disappointment in his eyes. Opening a door was still considered chivalrous in Texas.

They hadn't made it more than a few steps when the front door to the small green-siding bungalow popped open. A man who looked to be in his late forties or early fifties bounded out the door. He had on a variety of brightly colored prints and a matching cloth headband tied around his head. His hand was extended in front of him. He had a tanned, weathered face and a gap-toothed smile.

Grover had the whole Keep Austin Weird vibe down pat. He also looked like a bona fide hippie and she half expected him to offer them something besides the usual water or alcohol fare.

"How can I help you?" He looked at Dawson and then her. There was no hint of recognition.

Summer realized she had on a scarf, a ball cap and sunglasses. Her hair was tucked inside the hat as best she could. She removed a few articles and studied the man for any hint of recognition.

"Beautiful day," Dawson said, shaking Grover's hand. Dawson was stalling for time, waiting to see if Grover recognized her or him.

He looked from Summer to Dawson and back again before throwing his hands out to the side. "Would you like a tour of the wedding gazebo?"

The man looked confused when neither one of them answered.

"You married us a while back," Dawson began, and Grover really did seem caught off guard with the statement.

"Oh." He seemed to be searching his memory, trying to find a match to the couple standing in front of him. "I'm real sorry. I hope everything is okay with the—"

"It's all fine," Dawson reassured. "I was just hoping you could remember talking to my wife when you set up the arrangements."

Grover Hart seemed genuine enough, looking like he'd rather shoot the peace sign than anything else. He had flower child written all over him and she figured he was probably too high to remember much of anything most of the time.

"I could check my records if you'd like." He shrugged. His bushy eyebrows knitted together. "Was there something specific you were hoping I'd remember about the day?"

"No, I just thought you might recognize me. That's all," Summer said, figuring this was a dead end.

Dawson seemed to reach the same conclusion when he stuck out his hand and plastered on a smile. "Nothing to worry about here. We were driving by and thought we'd stop in and check with you. She lost her favorite earring on the day of the wedding and hoped you might remember seeing it. Since you don't, we'll be on our way."

Grover let out his breath like Dawson had just twisted a relief valve. She didn't think Grover was up to anything, but he did seem genuinely disappointed that he couldn't be of help.

"Thanks for trying," Summer said as she turned and headed toward the truck. Once inside, she said, "It's safe to say he didn't know my sister from Adam."

"I got the same impression." Dawson drove down the gravel lane, to the farm road leading to the highway. "Maybe we'll have better luck at the coffee shop."

She hoped.

The rest of the drive was quiet, save for the horns honking and general congestion of Austin where the term *rush hour* implied traffic actually let up at some point.

Using the map feature on her phone, it was easy to find Capital Coffee and not so easy to navigate downtown traffic, especially in a vehicle that took up much of the road.

By some miracle, Dawson found parking. The coffee shop was half a block away. It was midafternoon on a sunny day. Temperatures hovered around the midseventies.

He reached for her hand and laced their fingers together. His touch reassured her as she walked the downtown street with her glasses, hat and scarf. It was crazy to think Autumn had walked this same path countless times on her way to her favorite coffee shop.

It was reaching for another miracle that any of the employees would remember Autumn. Turnover in a coffee shop in a town with mostly college students had to be off the charts. Then again, maybe a good job with decent tips was hard to find.

For whatever reason, Autumn had come back to Austin after leaving Dawson. Summer could only think of one reason why her sister would do that... a man. Charley? Autumn was never the type to be alone and the divorce papers had Austin as the address of the 'lawyer.' She hated it and moved from relationship to relationship. Summer had hoped the marriage would stick, but now that she knew the details, she realized how naive she'd been to think her sister would've settled down.

Again, Summer was struck by how crazy her sister's actions had become over the past few years. She'd been straight-up crazy to leave Dawson. He was literally the perfect man.

Had she gotten herself into some kind of trouble? Autumn might have been lost and unpredictable but she'd never been one to break the law. Evidence would say otherwise, but Summer still knew her sister deep down. Autumn wasn't capable of doing much more than her little white lies.

A thought struck. How well could she say that she knew her sister? She was still scratching her head over Autumn leaving Dawson. Granted, her sister had built a mountain of lies—a mountain that she had to know would come tumbling down eventually.

She tugged at Dawson's hand for him to stop walking as she surveyed the street. "My sister had to know her lies would eventually catch up to her."

"It's possible they already were," he said, and she was already nodding. She'd been thinking the exact same thing.

Again, she couldn't for the life of her figure out what her sister had to lie about. "I've been thinking about what happens when people get married."

"Aside from the obvious part where they spend the rest of their lives together?" he asked.

"I'm thinking on a more practical level. The first thing people have to decide is whether or not to change their last names."

"Autumn was insistent on taking my name—"
He stopped cold.

"But she really wasn't. She only wanted people to *think* she was Autumn O'Connor."

Dawson was already nodding his head. "She wouldn't have to tell people her real last name if I believed we were really married."

"And we already know that the ranch is a safe haven. There's more security there than at the average bank." She didn't say Fort Knox even though she thought it.

"She never wanted to leave the property. A lot more makes sense about how squirrely she got when I tried to get her more involved in the plans to build. She kept saying that was my part. She only cared about the decorating."

"She might have been avoiding it because she had no plans to move into the house, after all."

"My thought exactly." There was no hint of regret in Dawson's voice. He spoke matter-of-factly about his past relationship with Autumn.

The realization gave her the sensation of a dozen butterflies releasing in her stomach.

"THIS EXPLAINS A LOT about her behavior." Dawson remembered how reluctant Autumn had been to commit to anything that had to do with the house or their future. At the time, he'd assumed her sadness about losing the baby was the cause. Now he realized she had been wriggling out of making those commitments possibly because she didn't want to stick him with her choices and her taste.

The strangest thing about the whole situation was that he would've done anything in his power to help her if she'd just asked. She didn't have to go through a fake pregnancy and a fake wedding to get him on her side. That was just how Dawson was made.

But it did make him think that she must not have

felt like she had another choice. Her lies stacked on top of lies. He was one hundred percent certain that he wasn't the only person she'd been lying to. Or rather, in the other case, lying to get away from.

Signs pointed to her doing something against the law or...

Dawson had come across plenty of types of liars in the course of his career. Most of the time, people lied to save their own behinds. Other times, they did so in order to save someone else's behind. He had to wonder which way it went with Autumn.

"Who am I looking for once we get inside the coffee shop?" Dawson motioned a few storefronts ahead where the sign read Capital Coffee.

"The guy at the coffee shop is tall and skinny. He has long, brown wavy hair that is usually pulled up in a man bun. He looks more like a local than a student to me. He seems to always have a red bandana tucked in the back pocket of his jeans that I don't think he ever uses." Summer's grip around Dawson's hand tightened as she gave the description.

Dawson hoped like hell this would be a lead. Otherwise, they'd driven a heck of a long way for nothing. He scanned the crowded sidewalk to see if anyone looked twice at Summer. They were at a distinct disadvantage considering this had been Autumn's stomping ground.

Summer might not realize who she was looking at and she could be staring into the eyes of her sister's killer. The worst part was that someone could mistake Summer for Autumn, just like what had happened the other day.

It had only been a few days, but they didn't seem any closer to figuring out who killed Autumn. He didn't have to remind his brother or anyone in law enforcement to keep the news of Autumn's death quiet, but he'd done it anyway.

Summer took the first step toward the coffee shop and Dawson kept hold of her hand. He also realized he'd know immediately if she recognized one of the men from yesterday based on involuntary muscle spasms. Her grip would tighten on his hand. He would have a couple extra seconds of warning with physical contact that he wouldn't have had otherwise.

He opened the door for her and followed her inside. The coffee shop was at the end of the street and had a fairly large outdoor space from what he could see. The temperature inside was no different than out.

Several hipster-looking waiters and waitresses moved through the crowded space. The inside of the coffee shop was relatively small. There was a long bar-height counter with a couple of people working the register and another pair manning the machines.

There were roughly a dozen tables. Several of them had two or three chairs nestled around them. There was a long green velvet sofa along one wall with several small laptop-friendly tables in a line. There were outlets galore.

Outside was impressive. There were more tables than he could count and lots of trees in planters. They hid people's faces. It was harder to stand at the front door and get a straight-shot look at everyone.

He took note of the other little nooks and corners. A couple of people in suits were hunkered over a table in one corner. There was pretty much every type of person in the coffee shop. The corporate types nestled around small tables and chatted. There had to be at least a couple of politicians, along with several political aids. At least one older gentleman had a hardback book the size of *War and Peace* in his hands as he sat with his legs stretched out and crossed at the ankles. His coffee mug sat on the table in front of him. He had that intellectual look with his sports coat and nylon slacks. He was most likely a professor at UT, which was a short walk from here.

Other than that, there were all manner of tattooed people milling about or at the chairs. Blue hair. Pink hair. Nose piercings. One lip piercing. Then, there was the usual crush of backpack-wearing students.

Dawson took it all in. He was used to sizing everyone up and evaluating all threat as a matter of habit. He knew where every exit door in the room was located.

Summer squeezed his hand. He glanced toward her and she nodded at a guy behind the counter. Man Bun was so busy manning the machines and frothing milk that he didn't bother to look up. He had an AirPod in one ear and seemed to be jamming out in a zone as he made orders and checked what looked like order ticker tape.

Time to see if Man Bun recognized Summer.

Chapter Ten

Dawson wanted to see Man Bun's unfiltered reaction to seeing Summer. He would be able to tell a lot about Man Bun's involvement or lack thereof in Autumn's death based on his initial reaction.

"I'm not sure how much I look like her like this. She never stepped out of the house without being all done up with full hair and makeup." Summer removed the glasses and ball cap. She fluffed her hair.

"In my opinion, the two of you don't look much alike. But there's enough of a resemblance to trick an acquaintance." He meant every one of those words. Autumn and Summer couldn't be more different as people. Summer had a warmth about her despite being very reserved. Autumn was more of an in-the-moment type. She had a bigger personality. The thought she'd been abused in her young life and that had caused her to become a bigger-than-life person on the outside with that same trapped little girl on the inside nearly gutted him.

Her defense mechanisms were well honed, and she'd had a lifetime to polish them. Knowing this

helped ease the frustration he felt from being burned
by her lies. Trauma could do that to a person. He'd
seen it too often in his line of work where someone
detached from society to protect themselves.

Those tendencies usually caused folks to fall into
the trap of abusing drugs or alcohol, sometimes both.
Based on what Summer had said so far, he believed
Autumn had developed an alternate persona instead.

It was a shame she'd had to do that in order to
survive their upbringing. He had even more respect
for Summer as he got to know her. She embodied
strength and probably a little bit of stubbornness, too.

Any survivor had to have a stubborn streak. Used
the right way, it could be very helpful because they
didn't give up once they set their mind to a goal.
Sometimes, that goal was simply not to let the past
break them.

It was a rare quality to have that kind of determination when it seemed the world was against a person. *She* was rare.

There was no arguing Summer Grayson was special.

She squeezed his hand before letting go, took in
a breath and then closed the distance to the counter. Standing right in front of Man Bun, she cleared
her throat.

Dawson stood back and to the side, pretending
to study something on the screen of his cell phone.

"Can I help y—"

Man Bun looked up. A hint of recognition passed
behind his eyes before he plastered on a smile.

Fake? Or was it the kind that people gave when they couldn't remember someone who obviously knew them?

"Hi. Remember me?" Summer plowed ahead through the awkward gaze. He had to give it to her. The stubborn streak made her strong when she probably wanted to bolt. The streak in her also meant justice was coming for her sister because Summer had the kind of tenacity normally seen in a starving pit bull going after a slab of meat.

Man Bun cocked his head to the side and squinted at her. This looked like he was trying to figure out if they'd dated or not. He gave the impression that she looked familiar but he couldn't place her.

"Autumn Grayson," she persisted.

Dawson scanned the room for anyone within earshot who took notice of the name. Nothing there. He sure as hell hoped this trip would be more productive in the investigation than it was turning out to be. He was about to take Summer to identify her sister's body. He couldn't think of a more awful thing for someone to have to do.

The only bright spot about this trip was supposed to be coming home with a lead to bring them one step closer to justice.

Man Bun threw his head back and smiled, genuine this time.

Dawson took a step closer to the counter so he could more clearly hear what Man Bun had to say.

"You remember me?" Summer did her best to sound perky. *Perky* wasn't a word he'd use to describe her personality. She was playing the part well, offering a bright smile as she put her hands up on the counter.

Dawson had no idea if she realized what that meant with her body language. But it was a show of trust, instinct at its finest, showing the person she was connecting with that she wasn't carrying any weapons.

"I do now." Man Bun stepped to the side where the counter was lower and nodded for Summer to follow. She did. He leaned across the smaller table like he was about to tell her a secret.

Dawson leaned a little closer and for reasons he didn't want to examine, the green-eyed monster reared its ugly head. He didn't like Summer getting anywhere close to Man Bun. The guy would be considered attractive by most. He looked like one of those celebrity soccer players from Latin America who made millions for his ability on the playing field.

"Where have you been?" Man Bun seemed to recognize Summer now.

"Around. You know how it is." Summer shrugged her shoulder, playing nonchalant.

"I almost didn't recognize you. Did you get a haircut?"

"How long has it been since the last time I was in here?" She paused, playing the ditz. She reached up and twirled a long strand of her wheat-colored hair. "I know it hasn't been so long that you would actually forget me."

Dawson stepped forward interrupting their conversation. He reached into his pocket and pulled out his wallet, flipping it open so that Man Bun would get a glimpse of his badge.

"How well do you know this person?" He nodded toward Summer.

Man Bun's eyes darted over toward someone on the line who was wearing a slightly nicer shirt and Dawson assumed was in management.

"Is that your boss?" Dawson followed the man's gaze.

Man Bun nodded. "One more strike and I'm out of a job."

"I can speak to him. This is official business."

"Nah, man. I don't want to make him suspicious. Just ask me what you want so I can get back on the line."

"How do you know Ms. Grayson?" Dawson asked.

"She's a regular. Comes in here all the time. Vanilla latte with whipped. It took me a second to recognize her because she looks different today."

"You talk to her a lot when she comes in?" Dawson asked.

"Sure." He shrugged his shoulder casually. "You know, when it's not busy. She's a good tipper and we like to treat our customers more like family."

Man Bun's eyes kept darting back toward his boss. Obviously, the guy was on his last strike and Dawson didn't want to be the reason he ended up without a job. The guy's answers were genuine and as much as Dawson wanted this to go somewhere, it wasn't going to.

"One last question. Did you ever see her come in here with anyone?" Dawson asked.

Man Bun looked at Summer as though she'd lost her mind. It was pretty obvious she was standing right there and his question was written all over his face, *Why not ask her?*

"She never really came in with anyone. Every once in a while, she would go outside, and I would lose track of her. People come in here all the time." He glanced around as though the crowded room was his proof. "As you can see, we're pretty busy."

He nervously glanced over at his boss and then the ticker tape machine that was kicking out orders. "If that's all, man, can I get back to work? My orders are stacking up."

"That's all I need for now. We'll be back in touch if we have more questions." Dawson produced a business card from his wallet. "If you think of anything else, I'd appreciate a call."

"Yes, sir." Man Bun's gaze bounced from Dawson to Summer and back. "Can I go now?"

Dawson nodded before reclaiming Summer's hand. He linked their fingers and turned to walk out the door.

Man Bun did an about-face. "Hey, now that I think about it there were a couple of dudes in here the other day asking around if anyone had seen her. I was thrown off a minute ago and forgot all about it."

"Can you describe what they looked like?" Dawson asked.

The descriptions fit the men Summer had encountered to a T.

"Have you ever seen them around before?" Dawson continued.

Man Bun shook his head.

"Thanks for the information."

Summer's hand tightened around Dawson's. She had a death grip on his fingers. The men who'd tried to attack her and who'd planned to kill her had come looking for Autumn in the coffee shop. The killer must not know Autumn was dead.

She didn't speak until they got outside, walked half a block and made sure no one was around to overhear their conversation. She'd already replaced the ball cap and sunglasses, and he could almost feel her heart racing through her fingertips.

"He was being honest, wasn't he?" she asked.

"I believe so. I didn't detect any deception in his behavior."

The disappointment on her face was a gut punch. He squeezed her hand for reassurance and his heart took another hit when she looked up at him with those big violet eyes.

"Then, we'll keep going until someone has information about her."

DEAD ENDS WERE EVERYWHERE.

Summer took in a deep breath as she and Dawson made their way back onto the highway and toward

Katy Gulch. The body suspected to have belonged to Autumn Grayson had, in fact, belonged to her sister. Decisions had been made about her sister's arrangements, despite the thick fog that had settled over Summer. Dawson had been a rock and she couldn't imagine doing any of this without him. The fact that he knew her sister at least on some level provided comfort. He seemed to genuinely care about what had happened to Autumn, despite her lies. That was the thing, underneath all those lies was a terrified person. The lies were like a wall that Autumn had used to keep everyone at a distance.

All Summer felt since was a deep dread and a sense of being completely numb. At some point, her brain might get to the point it could process what it had seen. Not without justice. Not without making those bastards pay.

Summer realized she'd been gripping the seat belt strap across her chest. At least she wasn't tapping the window. As far as nervous ticks went, hers were on full tilt.

About halfway home, Dawson's cell phone rang. He fished it out of his pocket and handed it over to her. "Do you mind checking to see who that is?"

She checked the screen. "It's your brother Colton."

"Would you mind answering and putting it on speaker?" Dawson's grip on the steering wheel was as tight as hers had been on her seat belt moments ago.

Obviously, seeing Autumn at the coroner's office was affecting him. He'd cared about her sister once.

He was a decent human being. And he was being incredibly understanding about Autumn's personality layers.

She pushed the button to put the call on the truck's speaker.

"Hey, Colton. You're on speaker and I'm in my truck with Summer Grayson."

"I look forward to meeting you at some point, Summer." There was not a hint of judgment in Colton's voice.

"Likewise," Summer said. She'd like to have the chance to meet all of Dawson's siblings. If they were half as decent and kind as Dawson, she couldn't think of a better caliber of men to be acquainted with. It was a foreign feeling to have one person who had Summer's back for a change. She couldn't even fathom having an entire support system in the form of a big family.

She'd never given much thought to having kids of her own. She always figured she'd get to a point financially where she could take care of herself and her sister. Open that small business they'd dreamed about. Then, she could think about a husband and possibly children down the road.

"What's going on?" Dawson asked his brother.

"Are you heading home?" Colton asked.

"On our way now," Dawson confirmed.

"You might want to make a U-turn."

Dawson navigated into the right lane and took the next exit. "What did you find out?"

"Gert has been doing some digging. You know Gert. Once she's on a scent, there's no stopping her."

Dawson glanced toward Summer. "Gert is his secretary."

Gert sounded like Summer's kind of person.

"I'm guessing she found something." Dawson said to his brother. His grip on the steering wheel tightened.

"It might be nothing, but it's worth checking into and I know you'll want to follow up on this yourself." Colton paused. "I apologize in advance for being frank with—"

"Please, don't worry about me. All I care about is justice for my sister," Summer said.

"Okay. Here's what Gert found. There was another strangulation victim in the Austin area. The tool used was a violin string. There was no DNA evidence in the case. The victim was twenty-eight years old and she had violet eyes."

"Same MO," Dawson muttered under his breath as he flipped on his turn signal and then banked a U-turn under the bridge.

Chapter Eleven

"I'll send you the file so you can take a look at witness statements." Summer wiped a stray tear as Colton continued, "It's a cold case."

She turned her face toward the passenger window like she was listening intently. In truth, she was trying to hold it together.

"How old is the case?" Dawson tapped his flat palm against the wheel.

"The murder happened two and a half years ago." The timeline could mean this guy moved on to Autumn. She might've gotten away and relocated to Katy Gulch to hide out where she met the one man who she believed could protect her. That would explain her wanting to stay on a secluded ranch and all the lies.

"What was her name?" Summer asked. She couldn't help herself. People in law enforcement would refer to her sister now as *the victim*. Summer wanted to know the young woman's name.

"Cheryl Tanning," Colton supplied.

Cheryl Tanning. She didn't deserve what happened to her, either.

"There were several suspects."

"Which one do you like?" Dawson asked.

"She used to frequent a coffee shop called Capital Coffee. Didn't you say you were visiting a place downtown that Autumn used to go to?" Colton asked.

Summer put her hand over her mouth to cover her gasp.

"We were just there," Dawson admitted.

In Summer's mind, the coffee shop would be a great place to scout a target for someone with an agenda. It was busy. All types of people came in and out. So much so, that people hardly noticed each other.

"So, it's the same place," Colton confirmed. "Okay."

"Is there mention of any other spots Cheryl used to hang out?" Dawson asked.

"That was the main place. There was a guy in her life, but her friends said she was very protective of him. No one knew who he was. A few names came up in the investigation. You'll see those in the file notes."

"I'll grab a place to stay. We might want to settle in for the night," Dawson said on a sigh. "I appreciate the information and tell Gert she did good work."

"She'll be tickled," Colton said before saying goodbye and ending the call.

The signs for Round Rock, a large suburb north of Austin, showed they were close to Austin again.

"Thought we might grab a place here for the night.

We can take a look at the files and then follow up on any discoveries. There's every kind of food imaginable, which I can pick up. I'd rather you be seen as little as possible while we investigate." There was so much warmth and compassion in his voice. "And now it looks like we need to circle back and visit the coffee shop again."

She couldn't agree more with what he said. There was no reason for her to be exposed more than necessary.

His cell phone buzzed and she assumed that meant the file was coming through.

"I have a laptop and an overnight bag in the backseat."

She quirked a brow.

"Don't always get a ton of notice when I have to head out. I keep most everything in the trunk of my sedan. The bag here is just for backup," he explained.

Her mind was still churning over what they'd just learned but she nodded. She was interested in hearing the details of his job. Staying focused when her mind was reeling proved harder than expected.

A serial killer? That couldn't be. How would she explain the two men chasing her yesterday if Autumn was killed by a serial killer? Hit men weren't serial killers and they usually didn't have henchmen.

Oh, Autumn. More of those fresh tears sprang to her eyes. She blinked them back. At least she felt something besides numb. Had her sister been in a relationship with a murderer and not realized it until

it was too late? What kind of person seduced his intended victims?

Dawson pulled off the highway and into a big
chain hotel. She straightened her baseball cap.

"I'll check us in and be right back." Dawson left
the truck idling and headed inside the lobby. He
was back a few minutes later, card keys in hand. He
slipped into the driver's seat and then pulled ahead
to a parking spot.

Summer kept her chin to her chest as she exited
the truck and waited for Dawson. He quickly grabbed
his emergency bag from the backseat before locking
up the truck and joining her.

He put his arm around her, shielding her from
other eyes. To onlookers, the move might seem intimate. A husband and wife stopping off at a roadside
hotel on their way somewhere else.

She knew he was covering as much of her as was
humanly possible. She was able to hide more of her
body and face.

Their room was on the fifth floor, number 510.
Dawson opened the door to the small suite. There
was a microwave and a mini fridge in the entryway
along with a coffee maker and an assortment of cof-
fees and teas. The bathroom was larger than the one
in her Washington apartment. The shower was trav-
ertine tile and the vanity area was large enough for
half a cosmetic store.

The main room had a work desk, a small table
with four chairs and a seating area. A flat screen TV
took up half the wall in the living room. There was a

comfortable if slightly worn sofa and two armchairs along with a marble coffee table.

This place was larger than her apartment back home. *Home*. Where was that anymore? Home was a foreign word to her now. Thinking about a future without Autumn was like walking forever in the dark, knowing light was out there in the distance but too far for her to see it.

Until she looked at Dawson and saw a glimmer of hope. Hope that she might somehow find her way through this darkness and toward the sun again. Hope that she might not want to spend the rest of her life alone. Hope she could have things she'd long ago dreamed about but never believed would be.

Anger seeded because she didn't want to think about a future that didn't involve her sister. Where did she even start?

"There's only one bed in the suite. It's yours. I can make myself comfortable here on the couch," Dawson said by way of explanation.

"That won't be a problem. I trust you. You can sleep in the same bed. I don't want to put you out." She was rewarded with a smile.

"It's no trouble." Dawson set his bag down, unzipped it and pulled out his laptop. He positioned it on the marble coffee table.

Summer moved next to him on the sofa and curled her left leg underneath her bottom.

"I want you to be prepared for the fact there are going to be graphic pictures. There's nothing wrong with skipping that part if you—"

She was already shaking her head. "I need to look at them. There might be something about her that reminds me of my sister. Something you wouldn't catch that I would."

Nothing in Summer wanted the images of a murdered Cheryl Tanning imprinted in her mind. But this was important. She would do whatever it took to find justice for her sister. This was the best way to see if there were any similarities.

He looked into her eyes like he was searching for confirmation it was okay to move forward. She gave him a slight nod before he fixed his gaze on the screen and opened a protected link.

There were two files in the one marked, Tanning Murder. The picture file contained two folders: evidence and victim. He clicked on the one marked Victim, and the screen was filled with thumbnails. He pulled up the first.

Cheryl Tanning's lifeless violet eyes fixed on a point above her. Her eyes were striking. Summer was always told that she and her sister had very rare-colored eyes. There was something haunting about the pair she was looking at.

Other than that, Cheryl Tanning was a beautiful young woman. She had pale skin and ruby-red lips. She had slightly darker hair than Summer and Autumn, and blunt-cut bangs. She was stunning. There was no question about that.

Dawson clicked on another photo and it was a full-body shot at the crime scene. Based on the photo,

"4 for 4" MINI-SURVEY

We are prepared to **REWARD** you with 4 FREE Books and Free Gifts for completing our MINI SURVEY!

Suspenseful Romance

Suspense

You'll get up to...
4 FREE BOOKS & FREE GIFTS

FREE Value Over $20!

just for participating in our Mini Survey!

Get Up To 4 Free Books!

Dear Reader,

IT'S A FACT: if you answer 4 quick questions, we'll send you 4 FREE REWARDS from each series you try!

Try **Harlequin® Romantic Suspense** books featuring heart-racing page-turners with unexpected plot twists and irresistible chemistry that will keep you guessing to the very end.

Try **Harlequin Intrigue® Larger-Print** books featuring action-packed stories that will keep you on the edge of your seat. Solve the crime and deliver justice at all costs.

Or **TRY BOTH!**

I'm not kidding you. As a leading publisher of women's fiction, we value your opinions... and your time. That's why we are prepared to reward you handsomely for completing our mini-survey. In fact, we have 4 Free Rewards for you, including 2 free books and 2 free gifts from each series you try!

Thank you for participating in our survey,

Pam Powers

To get your 4 FREE REWARDS:
Complete the survey below and return the insert today to receive up to 4 FREE BOOKS and FREE GIFTS guaranteed!

▼ **DETACH AND MAIL CARD TODAY!** ▼

"4 for 4" MINI-SURVEY

1 Is reading one of your favorite hobbies?

☐ YES ☐ NO

2 Do you prefer to read instead of watch TV?

☐ YES ☐ NO

3 Do you read newspapers and magazines?

☐ YES ☐ NO

4 Do you enjoy trying new book series with FREE BOOKS?

☐ YES ☐ NO

Please send me my Free Rewards, consisting of **2 Free Books from each series I select** and **Free Mystery Gifts**. I understand that I am under no obligation to buy anything, as explained on the back of this card.

☐ **Harlequin® Romantic Suspense** (240/340 HDL GQ5A)
☐ **Harlequin Intrigue® Larger-Print** (199/399 HDL GQ5A)
☐ **Try Both** (240/340 & 199/399 HDL GQ5M)

FIRST NAME	LAST NAME

ADDRESS

APT.#	CITY

STATE/PROV.	ZIP/POSTAL CODE

EMAIL ☐ Please check this box if you would like to receive newsletters and promotional emails from Harlequin Enterprises ULC and its affiliates. You can unsubscribe anytime.

© 2020 HARLEQUIN ENTERPRISES ULC
® and ™ are trademarks owned and used by the trademark owner and/or its licensee. Printed in the U.S.A.

HI/HRS-520-MS20

she looked to be about the same size as Autumn. Similar figures.

"This bastard likes a certain type." Dawson muttered a few more choice words under his breath.

She'd picked up on the similarities, too.

Her heart battered her rib cage as a weight dropped down around her arms. There was what looked like a wire wrapped around Cheryl's neck. They now knew it was a string from a violin.

What were the odds that Autumn would be killed by a similar method, two and a half years later? They had to be slim.

An icy chill gripped Summer's spine as she looked through the crime scene photos one by one. Dawson opened the case file next. A short description of the murder outlined that Cheryl Tanning had been found in an old dried up well on the back of someone's land. A group of teens who routinely rode dirt bikes on the property had stopped because of what they described as a smell that made them physically sick.

When they investigated, expecting to find an animal carcass, they received the shock of a lifetime when they found a body instead. All of the teens had been traumatized by the finding and during the course of the investigation had been cleared of any involvement.

There'd been a mystery man, who Cheryl's friends confirmed she'd been very secretive about.

"Do you think he was married?" Summer asked as she pointed to the screen.

"It's possible. A married man could have a lot to

lose if word got out that he was having an affair." Dawson confirmed.

"It's Austin, so my mind snaps to a married politician," she admitted.

"Can't be ruled out. But those aren't the only powerful men in the capital or men with something to lose if word of an affair got out. There are three things we look for in a murder investigation: means, motive and opportunity," he stated.

"Opportunity wouldn't be difficult in a secret affair. The person would be used to meeting one-on-one in possibly secluded locations," she reasoned.

"True. Affairs are sticky. She was hiding his identity and was protective of him, which gives me the impression he was the power broker in the relationship."

"Someone older than her? Someone smarter or more cunning? Someone used to getting exactly what he wants from people?" she asked.

"That's along the lines of what I'm thinking," he confirmed. "I'd add to that someone who stands to lose a lot, be it money, prestige or social standing if an affair is uncovered."

"A murder conviction would rock his world." She caught herself tapping her finger on the marble coffee table as her brain started working overtime.

"Attorneys, bankers, anyone with a professional license would be in jeopardy."

"Look here." Summer pointed to the screen. "It says at least one of her friends thought she was getting depressed. He blames the affair."

"The jerk could've been manipulating her, asking her to do things she didn't want to. She might've complied for fear of losing him."

Autumn could be a manipulator. But the shoe could easily have been on the other foot. She wasn't strong mentally, and when it came down to it, a person could exercise power over her.

CHERYL TANNING HAD no visible signs of molestation. There was no DNA left on her body or found on the scene. Nothing under her fingernails. No sign that she'd fought back.

She'd been secretly dating someone. There was nothing in her cell phone record that would indicate she'd been seeing someone. Her credit cards showed no unusual activity. At least one of her friends regretted teasing her about being a call girl, saying she started having a lot more cash than usual. The response had been that Cheryl stopped returning calls and texts for a while.

The strangulation came from behind. The method of killing was personal. The killer would have to have been literally standing right behind Cheryl. She didn't fight back, so maybe she thought her lover was playing a joke or trying to arouse her.

There were several bruises on Cheryl's body in varying stages of healing. She worked as a waitress and took night school classes. A waitressing job could explain the bruises on her thighs and arms. But so could sexual exploration.

A defense attorney might argue Cheryl Tanning

liked it rough in the bedroom. Or, at the very least, participated. Even if her lover had been identified, he wasn't necessarily guilty. Although, this kind of killing was personal. Staring at the evidence and the summary, Dawson was convinced the murderer was someone inside her circle despite the way the body had been dumped down the well.

The killer might have panicked. The police officer's report stated there'd been leaves tossed into the well after her body. Covering her up? Or covering her? As strange as it sounded, the sicko might have been covering her so she wouldn't get cold.

Dawson had seen enough deranged and sadistic people to last a lifetime. So, the leaves could actually be a sign of caring in a twisted way. Or a type of burial depending on religious affiliation. Even some cold-blooded killers believed they were spiritual. Hell, some killed out of ritual.

In this case, though, this bastard seemed well on his way to becoming a serial killer. The rule of thumb was three murders spread out over time.

If this killer believed that Autumn had lived, he would stop at nothing to silence her. There were all kinds of questions racing around in Dawson's mind.

"She didn't have a family, either," Summer noted.

"But Autumn did have a family. She had you."

"He didn't know that. Think about it, she hid me from you, too. I barely knew about you and the two of you were married." She made a good point. "Except that you weren't really."

"True." He rocked his head. "Then, that's part of his MO."

"Maybe he thinks no one will notice that they've gone missing and it'll give him more time to cover his tracks."

"I was thinking the same thing." Dawson pulled out the notepad and pen that he'd tucked into his emergency bag. He jotted down the fact the perp isolated his victims.

"Why did he decide to kill her, though?" she asked. "Like when did he know? The minute he started the affair?"

"It's possible. If Cheryl is his first victim, and so far Gert hasn't found any other that match this MO, he might have started the affair not knowing how it would end. At some point, he knew he was going to kill her."

"When he was done with her?"

"It's likely." He feared those words were like a physical blow. Of course, Summer would take them personally considering her sister was involved.

"My sister must've been scared of him. She might have felt backed into a corner with no way out," she continued.

It explained a lot about how she'd acted when he'd first met her and her actions after the fact. More of those puzzle pieces were clicking together.

"Do you think she figured out what happened to his former girlfriend?" she asked.

"It's highly possible."

"I just don't understand why she didn't go to law enforcement and explain her situation or tell me."

"Abusive men are master manipulators. He could've made her feel like he'd find her no matter where she went—"

"She could've come to me. I would've helped her find a way out of this."

"And she might think she would be bringing him right to your doorstep," he countered.

"The necklace. My name. You said it was one of her most prized possessions." Puzzle pieces were clicking together in her mind, too.

She tapped on the words they'd written on the notepad earlier. *Protect loved one.*

Chapter Twelve

A picture was emerging. Autumn had gotten into an unhealthy relationship that possibly even turned abusive. She didn't want Summer to know and so a couple of years ago, she withdrew.

The relationship became more than Autumn could handle. Luckily, she must not have told the guy about Summer. She'd kept her sister's identity safe and the necklace bearing her name locked in a box that she'd most likely kept hidden.

One day, Autumn decided enough was enough, or maybe things got heated between them and she began to fear for her life. Rather than go to Summer, and bring that blaze along with her, Autumn found a small town to hide in. Maybe she wanted to lay low.

Then, she met Dawson. He was honest and kind. It probably didn't hurt matters that he was smokin' hot. Maybe she even fell for him, fast and hard. He was everything she didn't have with the other guy.

There were perks to living with Dawson. He lived on a remote property and worked in law enforcement. As did several of his brothers. Autumn couldn't have asked for more or better protection. Her conscience got the best of her and she couldn't commit Dawson to an actual marriage, so she made up a pregnancy story, insisted on a low-key affair and then hired an internet guy who didn't care if proper papers were filed or not. It was a lot but sounded just like her sister to do something like this.

Summer relayed her theory to Dawson. It was met with nods of approval and that meant she was on the right path.

"The divorce makes no sense to me, though," she confessed.

"It was possible that he'd found her, or that she thought he would. She wasn't acting right in those last few weeks we were together. At the time, I chalked it up to her losing the baby. I tried to give her time and space to heal. I figured she would talk when she was ready but she just closed up. She stopped leaving the property and slept a lot of the time."

"Your logic sounds reasonable. Except that we both know there was no baby. So, he must've gotten to her somehow." How? was the question of the day. There was another bigger question…who?

"There were three suspects at the top of a short list in Cheryl's murder," Dawson said, pointing to the screen. "Sean Menendez, a creepy janitor, Jasper Holden, coffee shop worker and Drake Yarnell, ex-boyfriend."

"Okay. Where do we even start?" Something had been gnawing at the back of Summer's mind. She stared at the notebook page rather than the screen. Why was the name Charley bugging Summer?

"Is this exactly how my sister spelled the name, Charley? Just like it's written?" she asked Dawson.

"Yes. Why?"

She picked up the pen and wrote Cheryl next to Charley. "Does anything about this strike you as odd?"

"If I rearrange the letters and add an *a* the names are alike?" He rocked his head. "Look at that."

"She knew about Cheryl." That was the reason her sister was afraid. She knew about the murder.

"It's possible. She might have stumbled on a name and went to investigate. I can't imagine why she'd go back to Austin under the circumstances." Dawson tapped his finger on the screen. "We can start by interviewing Menendez, Holden and Yarnell."

More of those puzzle pieces Dawson had talked about before were being discovered. Finding where they fit and how they fit together was another story. Summer would take the progress. "I'm wondering why my sister went to the same coffee shop as Cheryl. Autumn didn't seem afraid to make her face known."

"It's possible she found evidence linking the murderer to the crime. If the perp found her in Katy Gulch, she had to know he would find her anywhere."

"Maybe he didn't know she'd found him out," Summer reasoned. "He could've convinced her to come back to Austin. Possibly even set her up in an apartment. Wine and dine her. She technically got away once. If this guy is a master manipulator, he might have convinced my sister that he loved her. He might have brought her back under his control."

Dawson nodded some more.

"He wasn't able to finish the job before. He wouldn't be able to let it go if he intended to kill her all along."

"What a sick bastard," Summer said.

"Agreed." The muscle in Dawson's jaw clenched.

"Then we're thinking that he lured her back in town." Summer hated the thought her sister could be manipulated. If the jerk said the right things, though, she could see her sister going back to him unless she knew he'd killed his other lover.

Autumn had had a knack for picking up guys who obsessed over her. At least until she'd met Dawson. He was the most levelheaded and down-to-earth person she'd ever met.

Summer hated all the secrets her sister held inside and all the lies. She hated that her sister couldn't just live a normal life and follow through on the dream of opening their own business. And she hated that she hadn't been able to protect her sister.

There was no use looking back now. A tidal wave of emotion was building inside Summer behind the wall that had kept her safe. There were cracks—cracks that threatened to pull her under and toss her around until she didn't know up from down anymore.

"You know, she wasn't always like this," she said on a sharp sigh.

"Tell me about it." Dawson clasped his hands together and rested his elbows on his thighs.

"The two of us were inseparable growing up. Our parents used to fight. I don't remember the details because we were so young when my father left. But I do recall feeling a sense of relief once he was gone."

"Kids pick up on so much. I've noticed it with my niece and nephew and they're only a year old. It's like a Record button has been hit in the back of their minds and someday, when they're much older, an invisible finger will hit Play. They won't even know why they're acting a certain way—it's just programming," he said.

"That's a really good point actually." Autumn had definitely recorded a lot of sadness. She seemed to take it more personally. "I can't say my sister even had good taste in the opposite sex." She flashed eyes at him, realizing how that would sound to him.

He feigned heartbreak before chuckling. "You really know how to hurt a guy's pride."

"Except for you," she quickly added.

"Right. Of course." Now he really laughed.

"No, seriously, I mean it. Don't take this the wrong way but I'm surprised you two were ever in a relationship. And what I mean by that is you're not normally her type. She always seemed to date guys who were edgy, you know, a little rough around the edges. Looking back, she always dated complicated people—a musician down on his luck or a guy in between jobs who needed her help. I used to always worry about her taste in men and told her she deserved better. Maybe that was part of the reason she came and found you. To protect her and show me that she was capable of finding someone who was amazing." She made the mistake of looking into his eyes as she said the last word.

DAWSON'S CHEST FISTED at the compliment. He couldn't afford to keep looking into those violet eyes without falling deeper into the well.

So, he coughed to clear his throat and asked, "What made you decide to work as a waitress?"

"I wanted to get experience in food service. I guess I saw it as my duty to take care of my sister and so we... *I*...dreamed of opening a small coffee shop together. Looking back, I did all the planning and talking about the coffee shop. She went along with it." There was a wistful quality to her eyes now. "She might not have wanted to hurt my feelings by saying she didn't want to open a business together."

"It sounds like you were trying to give her something to look forward to."

"True. I was. Now I'm wondering if I ran her off because I steamrolled over her."

"Don't do that to yourself. None of this is your fault."

"Oh, I doubt that. I should've done some—"

"I'm going to stop you right there. You didn't ask for this. You didn't contribute to this. As much as you might have felt responsible for your sister, you didn't do anything wrong. She had the will and the right to do whatever she wanted, and the person I knew did exactly that."

Summer paused and he hoped like hell she was letting his words sink in. This wasn't the first time she'd blamed herself for her sister's actions and if he could do anything else, he wanted to leave the impression with her that she didn't have to feel responsible. Adults were capable of making their own choices and did. Not all of those choices were good, and Autumn certainly made bad ones, but down deep, he didn't believe she was a bad person. Mixed up? Hell, yes. Confused? Absolutely. Bad? Not in his opinion.

"I hear what you're saying, and I know that in my mind. My heart is another story." She ducked her chin to her chest and turned her face away, a move he'd noticed she did to hide when she was getting emotional.

"It's okay to be upset. It's easy to see how much you love your sister. That's not going away and nothing will change that." He offered more words of comfort and when she turned to look at him, his heart took a dive.

She sat there, gazing at him, exposing her vulnerability to him. All he could offer by way of reassurance was a few words and his arms. He looped his arms around her, and she buried her face in his chest.

They stayed in that position for a long time. When she was ready to pull back, he feathered a kiss on her forehead. Being together with Summer like that, vulnerabilities exposed, was the most intimate moment in Dawson's life.

"Thank you." Her voice was shaky despite her chin jutting out.

"I'm here anytime. I mean that, Summer." He did. He meant long after this case was behind them and the grief settled in. Long after they were gone from this hotel room, from Austin and back into their normal everyday lives. He wanted to be there for her.

Summer and her sister didn't seem to have had a whole lot of breaks in life. He regretted that he'd missed so many signs with Autumn, but he would be there for Summer anytime she needed a friend.

"You can't know how much I appreciate it, Dawson." He could tell by the way she said those words she had no plans to take him up on his offer.

Why did that sting so much?

"So, Charley could possibly mean Cheryl." Summer brought the conversation back on track. "Which meant my sister either knew about Cheryl or heard the name."

Dawson nodded. "We're missing the connection, if there is one. Since you don't know much about your sister's daily habits, it's difficult to figure out where her and Cheryl's lives might have overlapped."

"That's true. It's interesting to note that Cheryl doesn't have any relatives who she was close to." Summer frowned and he immediately realized why. "So, they have that similarity. And we know that they both visited the same coffee shop. Maybe they lived near each other. Maybe that's another link. So, the perp lives or works in the area of the coffee shop."

Dawson wrote the question down on the pad of paper: "Did they live near each other or possibly know each other?"

"We know they looked alike and spent time in the same area of town. They might have had a few other touch points."

"Your sister left the money I gave her in the bank. She never touched it. I still can't figure out why. She must've needed it," he said.

"Unless she went somewhere she didn't, which would mean she left you to go back to the perp."

"Why?"

Good question. One he intended to find an answer to.

Dawson didn't realize how late it was getting and neither one of them had really slept last night. He'd be fine running on a few minutes of sleep here and there but Summer looked absolutely wrung out. She needed food and rest.

"What do you think about taking a break and grabbing some dinner?" he asked.

"I seriously doubt I could eat anything," she countered.

"Would you be willing to try?" It was important and she might surprise herself like she had with the meatloaf.

"I probably should but I don't want to be alone right now." Her violet eyes pleaded.

Taking her with him carried risks. One could

argue leaving her alone in a hotel room also left her vulnerable. The mental debate going on in his head was a force to be reckoned with and yet he knew in his heart he couldn't leave her there alone.

He thought about ordering food and staying in. That could draw unwanted attention and expose them should someone be watching the room. It was dark so the sunglasses wouldn't work. That, too, would draw attention. Granted, Autumn had always been done-up with full makeup and her hair done to the nines, and Summer went with an all-natural look. It was possible the perp could recognize her.

"You could wrap the scarf around your hair," he said.

She was on her feet faster than he could say, "Boo."

Her violet eyes were red rimmed. He wanted her to know how brave she was. Most would buckle under the circumstances and yet she kept pushing forward, searching for answers for her sister.

When she was finished covering her hair, he linked their fingers and walked with her outside. Glancing around, the hair on the back of his neck stood on end. Not exactly a warm and fuzzy feeling, but he was on high alert.

The feeling persisted during the entire walk to the truck. Again, he put his arm around her to shield her as much as possible from view. Being this close to Summer, breathing in her clean and flowery scent, filled his thoughts with the kisses they'd shared.

Under different circumstances, she was exactly

the kind of person he'd want to spend time getting to know better. Now?

It was complicated. His feelings were complicated. And despite their off-the-charts attraction, acting on it any further would make things between them even more complicated.

And the crazy thing was that a very huge part of him didn't want to care about the consequences.

Chapter Thirteen

The restaurant was one of those taco chain spots found in every major Texas city. Loud music was playing when they entered and, unlike everyone else, she didn't love tacos. They were okay. Edible.

Summer pointed toward the booth in the corner where she and Dawson could continue talking about the case. The images of Cheryl Tanning would haunt Summer for a very long time. Erasing those wouldn't be easy.

And her mind drew the parallels to her own sister's case. Obviously, the bastard had killed Autumn in a similar way. It was impossible not to imagine Autumn's face instead of Cheryl's.

She'd tucked the notebook and pen under her arm before leaving the hotel room, just in case they wanted to jot down more notes. She placed the items on the table and scooted them toward the wall in case a server brought their order.

One word jumped out at her. *Suspects.* Below the word, there were three names. Dawson had explained that law enforcement officers had interviewed everyone they could find. Cheryl Tanning might not have had a family to stand up for her but she'd had a voice in the detective who had taken the case.

"Drake Yarnell, what do you think of him?" she quietly asked Dawson.

"He was an ex-boyfriend who was in a biker club. He had a jealous streak and I didn't like that at first. But the timeline of their relationship ending? They'd broken up almost a year prior. I doubt he still had the kind of feelings or possessiveness required to circle back and murder his ex-girlfriend."

"Even though their neighbors overheard him threaten to kill her if she walked out the door when they lived together?" she asked.

"He was a hothead. I can't see him waiting almost a year to act on his threat. It was idle, said in the heat of the moment. I still want to talk to him but he isn't sending up any red flags to me so far."

"Okay. How about Sean Menendez?"

"He was the creepy maintenance worker in her apartment complex." Dawson tilted his head toward her and then looked down at the pad of paper.

"Right."

"It's possible he had a thing for her and even more possible he was stalking her. Going down that path, she rebuffed him and that's the reason the detective thought he was a good suspect." Dawson made a face.

"You don't think so."

"Not really. Why would anyone cover the body

with the leaves? And what's the connection to the violin strings?" he asked.

"This detective believed he might've found the strings in one of the trash bins," she stated.

"Which makes sense and would be possible. But then, what about your sister? How is she connected to the apartments and this guy? Did she live there? He's a creep, don't get me wrong. If I was a beat cop, I'd be keeping an eye on him. But, I can't connect him to Autumn and we're banking everything on these two cases being connected." His lips formed a thin line.

The waiter brought their taco baskets, so they tabled the discussion for the moment. The minute he left, they started up again.

"So, Jasper Holden? What are your thoughts about him?" she asked.

"He was a server at the coffee shop and that meant he would know both of the victims. He might not *know* them but he was acquainted with them both. Or at least, we think he was. He would've seen both of them coming and going, except that they might not have been there at the same time," he said. "He was a biochemistry major, which meant he was smart."

"Did he graduate by now?" she asked. It might be harder to track him down if he'd moved on. People came from all over Texas and beyond to attend UT in Austin. It wasn't an easy school to get into and a major like biochemistry would be even harder. Jasper would've had to have been pretty brilliant to pull that off. She wondered if he'd played in his high school band.

"I can't remember off the top of my head if he was a junior or senior at the time of Cheryl's murder. Could rule him out if he'd graduated and moved away at the time of Autumn's murder."

"There's another thing that's been bothering me about my sister. How did she have money for things like coffee? As far as we know she didn't have a job. And she didn't touch the money you put in the account for her." The fact he'd done that despite how her sister had treated him was above and beyond honorable.

"It's possible she had a job. The coroner's office had very few of her personal belongings. No purse, no wallet and no cell phone. It's a big part of the reason he was having trouble identifying her."

"And also unheard of not to carry those items around everywhere. I can't live without my cell." She nodded toward her purse.

"We could talk to the detective in the Tanning case. She might be able to give us insight into Jasper's current whereabouts."

"That seems like a good idea," she agreed.

"She also seemed especially thorough in Cheryl's investigation. It signals to me that she didn't want to give up on the case."

"What do you think happened?" Summer must've been hungrier than she realized because she finished off the beans and rice that came on her plate alongside her pair of tacos.

"Austin's a fairly large city with higher crime rates than what we see in smaller towns. These things generally come down to available resources. Detective Libby was most likely pulled from the case when she stopped making progress. She might've worked it on her lunch breaks or after hours but eventually leads dry up."

Summer shivered. An icy chill ran down her spine. The thought that Cheryl Tanning had died alone nearly broke Summer's heart. Their lives were not so different now. It wasn't like there was anyone at home waiting for Summer. No life that extended much beyond a small group of coworkers at the diner who she spent hours on end with but barely knew on a personal level.

Actually, that wasn't entirely true. She knew about Marta's boyfriend who revved his motorcycle engine out front to signal he was ready to pick her up after her shift was over. She knew that Dane, one of the cooks, had tattoos running up both arms. He used to joke that he'd gotten them so no one would try to chat him up in line to get his morning coffee. He was the biggest teddy bear once she got to know him.

Summer, on the other hand, shared very little about her private life with her coworkers. She'd always seen the diner as a temporary stop, a place she shouldn't get too comfortable. She'd always played her cards close to her chest, sitting quietly in the breakroom while the others talked about weekend plans or bills due.

She'd gotten so good at keeping everyone at a distance, not unlike Cheryl or Autumn. Cheryl probably had goals. She was probably working toward something when her life had been cut short. Everyone had a dream. Didn't they? Everyone deserved to live out their potential.

Seeing two lives cut so drastically short sent a hot, angry fireball through her veins. Her eyes were too dried up to cry. She let those tears flow earlier in sweet release.

The anger motivated her to find answers. If Sean Menendez wasn't the killer, or Jasper Holden, or Drake Yarnell, Summer wouldn't stop until she figured out who was. The small amount of money she'd socked away for the business would be enough to get by. She'd been afraid to turn up at the bank after the jerks had chased her.

An idea struck.

"I could draw him out, Dawson."

"We talked about this before. This bastard isn't getting within five feet of you."

"Think about it. I could hang out at the coffee shop. My sister used to go there and so did Cheryl. That means this jerk might go there, too," she countered.

"Yeah? What if that's true. Do you really want to walk right into his hands?"

"I could dress up like my sister—"

"I think the words you're looking for are *a sting operation* and it would be way too risky. No responsible law enforcement officer would use you as bait to bring out a deranged killer and I might not be able to cover you from every angle. He knows what you look like, which puts us at a huge disadvantage."

"You're right." She needed to do something. Sitting here, doing nothing, would drive her insane.

"We have to be patient."

IMPATIENCE ROLLED OFF Summer in waves. Dawson understood. They were still studying the facts of the case and it wouldn't feel like they were making any progress to her. The way she was twisting her fingers together, picking up her food just to put it down before eventually taking a bite told him that her nerves were on edge.

It was easy to feel like they were spinning their wheels at this stage of the investigation. They were making progress, though. Slow, steady progress. Inch by inch but he'd take it. They had a similar and linked case to work with. It was a lot more to work with than what they'd had twelve hours ago.

Getting a strong lead with no real break was frustrating. Dawson had been involved in enough investigations over the years to know not every case was solved. As sad and frustrating as it was, there were times when the trail went so cold there was nothing left to follow.

And yet, he couldn't let himself think they wouldn't find the truth. Besides, they had a secret weapon. They had Colton and Gert back in Katy Gulch. Once Gert latched on to a case, her nickname quickly became Pit Bull.

The name responsible for Cheryl's and Autumn's murders were not in that file. Dawson was almost one hundred percent positive, which didn't mean he wouldn't retrace Detective Libby's tracks. He had every intention of interviewing Jasper Holden, Drake Yarnelle and Sean Menendez. Dawson never knew when a seemingly insignificant piece of evidence or interview might blow the case wide-open.

When he glanced over at Summer and realized she'd cleaned her plate and was studying the paper that contained their notes like it was the night before a final exam, he knew it was time to go. Her finger tapped double time on the wood table, a sign her stress levels were hitting the roof again.

The waiter stopped by the table and asked if they needed anything else.

"Just the bill," Dawson said, noticing how much the good-looking waiter kept staring at Summer.

She was beautiful, and he'd noticed most men checked her out when she walked into a room. Not exactly easy to keep her on the down low. Dawson tried to convince himself that was the reason their stares burned him up and not because a piece of him—a growing piece at that—wanted them to stake a claim on each other.

The waiter disappeared, returning a minute later with the bill. Dawson always carried cash. He never knew when he would need it on the road or in a small town, so he'd learned to keep a small stash with him at all times. This was one of the times he was grateful for the habit because he was ready to get her back to the hotel and out of plain view.

He wrapped his arm around her as they headed out the door, again noticing how right she felt in his arms. Again, ignoring the part of him that wanted this to be permanent.

It was dark outside and would be easier to move around at night without risking her. Most of the time, his witnesses were moved under the cover of night. Of course, it all depended on where he was going. Night in a big city still bustled with activity and no one really paid much attention to each other after a quick, primal is-this-person-a-threat-to-my-safety check.

Clean-cut couples barely hit the radar. That was always a good thing in Dawson's line of work and generally the goal. Colton had been in touch with Detective Liddy to let her know about the connection to Autumn and what they were now investigating. Dawson had to follow the right channels.

"I want to make a pit stop before heading back to the hotel." He'd scratched down Drake Yarnell's address on the notepad.

"Oh, yeah?" Summer's face lit up and he wondered if she realized how much danger she was in, *still* in, despite being with a US marshal.

"Yarnell lives in downtown, on the southwest side of Austin. I'd like to swing by his last known address. Detective Libby wrote down that he'd taken over the family home once his mother passed away five years ago. I'm thinking it's a safe bet he still lives there if the house is paid for. Holden and Menendez could be more mobile, especially Holden." They already knew one was a college student and the other worked at the apartment complex where Cheryl lived. A few years after the fact, he might've moved on. It was a safe bet he would stay in the same line of work but that didn't mean he would be at the same place of employment.

She nodded quietly and he wondered what was going through her mind. It took him a second to register that she would be wondering if she was about to come face-to-face with her sister's killer.

He walked her to the passenger side of the truck, and opened the door. Not because he didn't think she was capable of doing it for herself, but it was part of that cowboy code that required putting others first. It was a tradition well rooted in a Texan and one he hoped would never die.

Aside from being ingrained in him, it was protection for Summer. The less she was visible, the better.

He ignored the fact that he liked being in constant physical contact with her.

Chapter Fourteen

The southeast area of Austin's downtown was a row of bungalow-style houses in various states of disrepair. Rentals to university students—the kind who used lawn furniture inside the house and might have a keg on tap at all times but no food in the fridge—ensured the area was prone to crime.

As always, there were a few residents who'd decided to stick it out and whose social security checks or pensions weren't enough to cover new sod when needed or paint.

It was an interesting mix on Fourth. There was a steady wail of sirens in the background and, despite being what most might consider a rough area, an almost constant stream of foot traffic regardless of the late hour.

He pulled the truck up to the house across the street from Yarnell's place and pointed. "His is that one."

The porch light wasn't much more than a bulb hanging from a wire, and it kept blinking. Not exactly a good sign for stable electricity. He reminded himself to ask Yarnell to step outside. Getting fried by electrical current wasn't high on his list of favorite things.

Lights were on inside the house. Didn't necessarily mean Yarnell himself was home but someone had to be. One of the lights in the front window turned off. Proof someone was moving around.

The front door opened, and a big burly guy stepped out.

"Wait here," Dawson requested as he hopped out of the driver's seat. The person's back was to him. The guy wore a black leather jacket with a massive orange logo covering the entire back. It explained the motorcycle parked in the front yard and they already knew Yarnell was a biker from Cheryl's case file.

Dawson crossed the street and made it to the metal fencing with overgrown scrub brush winding through the slats.

"Excuse me," he said.

Motorcycle Guy turned his head to one side but didn't look at Dawson. "Can I help you?"

"I hope so. I'm looking for Drake Yarnell." This guy fit the physical description of five feet eleven with a stocky build. His arms were covered by the jacket so Dawson couldn't tell if there were tattoos. But then, tattoos in Austin were commonplace so they didn't exactly stand out necessarily as an identifier. According to the files, Yarnell had a snake winding up his left arm, the tail of which stopped at the middle finger on his left hand. Now that was distinctive.

Dawson's question got the guy's attention. He slowly turned, looking ready for a fight. Dawson noticed his right hand fisted around his key. There was no reason to poke the bear.

"You found him."

Yarnell had grown a beard and mustache since the photos of him were taken two years ago. He looked like he'd aged more than two years but hard living could do that and, based on the condition of his home, it looked like he was doing just that. There were empty beer cans littering the yard. Dawson wasn't sure he wanted to know what else was.

"I'm a friend of Detective Libby's. My name is US Marshal Dawson O'Connor." He pulled out his wallet and produced his badge.

Yarnell's dull blue eyes widened. His skin was sun-worn, his hair a little too long, and it looked like he'd just gotten off tour with a heavy metal band with a red bandana keeping his hair out of his eyes.

"I told the detective I wasn't involved then and nothing's changed, man." Yarnell put his hands in the air, palms out, in the universal sign of surrender. "But I hate that Cheryl's gone and hate the bastard that killed her."

"Good. Because I'm here in the hopes you can help us find him and lock him away forever."

"I'd like to help out but I'm late for work. You know how it is." If Yarnell was waiting for Dawson to ask him to schedule an appointment and give another statement he had another think coming.

"All I need is a couple minutes of your time," Dawson said.

Yarnell glanced at his watch before glaring at Dawson. "I'll do it for Cheryl. But, damn, I thought this whole thing would go away by now."

There was a weariness in Yarnell's voice that said he'd been put through the ringer. He'd been the prime suspect for a while according to the file. His shoulders deflated and it looked like the wind was knocked out of him.

"Not until her killer is behind bars," Dawson said, matching Yarnell's intensity.

"Fair enough." Yarnell relaxed his hand by his side. "What do you want to ask me that can't be found in my statement or in the files?"

"There's been another murder." Dawson figured coming out with the truth was the best way to gain Yarnell's cooperation.

"Who?" Yarnell asked.

"Autumn Grayson. Do you know her?"

Yarnell shook his head. His response was instant, which made Dawson believe the man was telling the truth.

"Do you think I did it?"

"No. But, to be honest, I would've interviewed you, too. Possibly more than once. Because Cheryl deserves justice and in talking to you, I might have found a clue." Using her first name would bring this conversation onto a personal level. It was personal, too. Any time a life was taken, it was personal for Dawson.

Yarnell's gaze traveled over Dawson like he was sizing him up for a fight.

"Good," he finally said. "Because she didn't deserve what happened to her."

"How did you first hear about the murder?" Dawson asked.

"When four cops showed up at my house with a battering ram," he stated matter-of-factly. "No one seemed to care that we'd been broken up for a while. I'd thought she was cheating on me and I said some things I shouldn't have. An older couple used to live next door and they were always calling the law on me. I guess my shouting at her gave them ammunition."

Dawson already knew Yarnell didn't retaliate against the neighbors. No additional reports had been filed against him despite the fact he'd been watched like a hawk.

"I'm a day late and a dollar short but I care about your history with Cheryl. When the two of you broke up, did you have any proof she was seeing someone else?"

"Nah, just a suspicion. She started acting weird. Secretive. She would disappear for a morning and get offended if I asked where she'd gone." He tucked his hands in his pockets. "Hell, I was just curious at first but after a while I started to think something was up. She would tell me she had to work an extra shift at the hospital where she checked patients in and then I'd show up to surprise her with dinner but her coworkers said she wasn't on the schedule. She got real upset about me going to her job."

"Did you stop?"

"Yeah." He shrugged. "I'm not going to lie. I waited out in the parking lot for her a few times with my lights off. I got caught by the night guard once and he threatened to turn me in if I did it again."

"Was that the end of it?"

Yarnell shrugged. "I'm not proud of the fact now but I used to drink and I waited for her more than once across the street from the hospital. She always parked in the south lot. I'd cruise through with a friend to see if her car was there."

"Was it?"

"Sometimes. Others not so much. She would make up some lame excuse about having to leave early. I guess she got tired of all the questions and moved out."

"She lived with you here?"

"For a few months. She didn't have enough saved up for her own place. She needed first and last month's rent, which was pretty steep. So, she stayed here and cooked instead of pitching in for rent. My roommates weren't crazy about it at first but they got over it. It's my house."

Dawson nodded. The report never said she'd lived with Yarnell. The detective must not have thought the fact was important. He couldn't say he would agree with the assessment and it also indicated a sloppier investigation than he would've liked to see.

"Over the course of your relationship, were you

ever physically violent with Cheryl? While you were drinking?" He added that last part after catching the look of disappointment in Yarnell's eyes. He seemed like the kind of guy who'd partied a little too hard and became something he wasn't proud of. The report said he couldn't hold down a job and Dawson wondered if the drinking was a big part of that.

"I left marks on her arms a couple of times from grabbing her too hard. If you're asking if I roughed her up, the answer is no. She did come home with bruises sometimes. It got worse after she moved out. Suddenly, she had enough money to pay the deposit on her apartment. I stayed over once or twice and there was cash in her nightstand—"

Again, Yarnell put his hands in the surrender position.

"Hey, I was just looking for a condom. I wasn't rooting through her stuff like some crazed stalker."

"When was the last time you saw Cheryl?"

"Alive or dead?" He was goading now, understandably angry at having to dredge up what must've been a painful past.

Dawson didn't respond. There were times when it was a good idea to shut someone down and remind them to be respectful and there were times when the law had chewed someone up and spit them out on the other side. Yarnell would pull it together if given a minute to regain his composure. His stress level was through the roof and he looked like he was about to blow. He needed a release valve. In this case, a few minutes to blow out a sharp breath and reset was all it took.

He covered his mouth with his hand, a move someone did right before they were about to lie. In this case, though, he seemed like he didn't want to say the words he had to say next.

"I saw dead pictures of her. The detective, the blonde…what was her name again?"

"Libby."

"Right." He blew out another breath and looked up to the stars. "The Big Dipper."

"Excuse me? I'm not following."

"It was Cheryl's favorite. She pointed it out every time we went outside at night. She would stop in the middle of the street and search for it." He hung his head. "I can't count the number of times I had to pull her out of the road before she got hit by a car."

Dawson had seen this before in investigations. The person interviewed needed to remember something good about the deceased. The memories just bubbled up and it was like they had to come out. Remembering was a good thing. It connected Yarnell to Cheryl's memory. It would rekindle his anger that her life had been cut short.

"I can't say that I remember anymore. Whatever I said in the report is right. It had been months since I'd seen or heard from Cheryl, but I lost track of how many." He glanced down at an empty beer can with a deep longing. Like he needed one of those but couldn't because of work.

"The report says she called you a week before

her murder. The call lasted forty seconds," Dawson pointed out.

"My girl answered when she saw my ex's name. She said a few choice words and Cheryl never tried to call back. Detective Libby brought that up a lot before. She swore I was lying but it's the truth. I never spoke to Cheryl before…" His voice broke on that last word and he turned his face away before clearing his throat and regaining his stiff composure. "I never got a chance to say goodbye."

Drake Yarnell's suffering could be seen in his weary eyes. "What if she was calling for help or to get back together. If she'd come back to me, I could've taken care of her."

It was easy to see Yarnell cared for Cheryl and that he'd been racked with guilt ever since her death.

Dawson brought his hand up to Yarnell's shoulder in a show of comfort. "You didn't know what was about to happen. There's no way to go back and undo the past. Try to make peace with it if you can."

"I appreciate that, bro." Yarnell seemed genuine and his honesty touched Dawson. One of the bright spots in his job was being the one to help someone see a tragedy wasn't their fault or helping a family find answers or justice.

He was frustrated that he hadn't been able to do that for Summer, or for Autumn for that matter.

"If you ever need to talk." Dawson pulled a business card out of his wallet. "I'm around."

Yarnell looked Dawson in the eye like he couldn't believe his ears.

"That's cool, bro. Uh, thanks."

What was the point of his job if he couldn't help people? He was usually picking up some lowlife with a felony warrant who'd evaded law enforcement and was considered dangerous. Yarnell had made mistakes in his past and Dawson would never condone being physical with the opposite sex.

He did, however, believe in second chances if any person was serious about cleaning up his or her act.

"I'm serious. Use it."

"I will." Yarnell took the offering. Those dull blue eyes held a momentary spark of hope—hope that he might get some relief from the hell he'd been living in since the dark day Cheryl was murdered.

This was the hell of investigations. A suspect who was innocent. The toll it took on a person's life.

"I'll let you get to work on time."

Yarnell nodded and tucked the business card in the inside pocket of his leather jacket. As Dawson left the yard, he accidentally stepped on a beer can, crushing it with his boot. He kicked the can aside before making his way back to Summer.

"He's innocent. There's nothing more to get out of him," Dawson said as he reclaimed his seat. He'd left the keys in the ignition in case Summer had needed to make a quick getaway.

"I'm wondering if the coffee shop is still open. Maybe we could stop by there and ask around for Holden."

He glanced at the clock as he navigated down the small residential street. There was barely enough

room to get through with cars parked on the street
and being in his truck wasn't helping. This part of
Austin had the most narrow streets. He was used to
it, having been here countless times to apprehend a
criminal. But it was making Summer nervous based
on her expression as he squeezed through.

As he turned on his blinker and pulled up to the
light of a busy intersection, Summer gasped.

She pointed her finger at a guy who was walking behind a young woman. She seemed to be alone.
Earbuds in, she didn't seem to be paying attention
to her surroundings.

"That's him. That's one of the guys who was chasing me the other day," Summer said.

Chapter Fifteen

Summer's pulse raced as adrenaline pumped through her veins. She flexed her fingers a few times, trying to release some of the pent-up nerves as she sat ramrod straight in her seat. The guy who'd almost grabbed her stared at the back of the head of the woman walking ahead of him.

Thick Guy's arms extended, his focus laser-like, about to grab the unaware young woman. An icy chill raced through Summer and an involuntary reflex caused her to shout. No one would hear her inside the truck with the windows rolled up.

Dawson cut over to the other side of the street, and then pulled alongside the curb. He was out of the truck before Summer had a chance to take her seat belt off. The burst of adrenaline that put her body on high alert also caused her hands to shake.

She fumbled with the clasp but finally got the thing off. It pulled back with a snap against the door, but she was already shoving her shoulder into the door to open it.

Summer was out of the vehicle and gunning toward

the young woman in seconds. She stumbled over the curb and nearly face planted. Taking a few steps to right herself, she glanced up in time to see a sneer on Thick Guy's face. Another chill raced down her back.

Thick Guy's gaze bounced to Dawson. A look of shock and then anger crossed his features before he turned and bolted in the opposite direction. For a sturdy guy, he had a superfast gait. Dawson turned up the gas and was right behind the perp.

The young woman glanced around and seemed to realize what had been about to go down. Her mouth fell open, her eyes widened and her skin paled. She tapped the white bud in her ear and started crying.

"You're okay," Summer soothed as she wrapped the young woman in an embrace. "Nothing happened. You're fine."

The young woman bawled in her arms. Summer was keenly aware that Thick Guy had had an accomplice last time. She scanned the area, searching for Scrappy. She also keenly realized she and the young woman were alone. Dawson had disappeared down the dark street.

"What's your name?" Summer asked, trying to get the young woman to focus on something besides what had almost just happened.

"Harper."

"Here's what we're going to do, Harper. We're going to go into my friend's truck and wait for him. Don't be scared. He works in law enforcement," she said as calmly and evenly as she could.

"Okay," came out through sobs.

Harper looked to be no older than nineteen. Summer walked the young woman over to the truck and locked them both inside.

"Do you live around here, Harper?" Summer asked.

"No." Harper shook her head. "I was walking to the UT shuttle after a study group meeting a few blocks away from here."

There were bus stops all over the city for UT students.

Right about then, Summer caught sight of Thick Guy walking toward them. Head down, hands behind his back, he looked to be in handcuffs. He heaved for air.

Dawson shoved him across the hood of the truck and wiped blood from his busted lip. Panic washed over Summer at the thought anything could happen to him. She reminded herself that he was standing right there, on his phone, most likely calling in what he'd seen so Thick Guy would be taken in.

Face down, Summer couldn't see Thick Guy's face. But she knew it was him. He had the same height and build. The same black hair. He turned his head to the side and tried to look through the windshield. She caught a glimpse of those same dark eyes.

"Is that him?" Harper asked even though the answer was obvious. She was practically hyperventilating.

"Yes. He's handcuffed and going to jail." If not for what he was about to do to Harper, then what he'd almost done to Summer.

Was hers a random attack? There was no way. She distinctly remembered him and his friend talking about Autumn. What had they said? *She just won't die.*

Summer couldn't imagine her sister getting involved with Thick Guy or Scrappy. Were they for hire? Had Thick Guy seen a pretty young coed walking down the street and decided to take one for himself?

She shivered and her skin crawled at what could have just happened to Harper.

"I need to call my roommate and let her know that I'm going to be late." Harper's voice sounded small and scared.

"Okay. Where's your phone?" Summer asked when Harper didn't immediately make a move.

"My backpack." Harper shrugged the floral-patterned quilt-like material backpack off her shoulder. She unzipped it as tears streamed down her face.

"Hey, he didn't get to you. You're going to be all right. You're safe." Summer looked into Harper's eyes, willing her to be strong. She looked even younger with red, puffy eyes.

"Thank you for stopping. I didn't even hear him over my music, and he must have been right behind me."

"He's done this before. He didn't want to be heard," Summer said.

"I don't know what I would've done if you hadn't shown up when you did."

Summer didn't want to think about it. Thick Guy seemed strong. Harper probably didn't weigh more than a hundred pounds wet. She was five feet two inches in heels.

"Call your roommate so she doesn't worry. We'll give you a ride home," Summer said. She doubted Dawson would mind that she'd made the offer.

Harper made the call and got through it with a few more sobs. Her roommate promised to be home and to wait up for her. Summer was relieved the young woman wouldn't be alone. She would be experiencing the effects of that trauma for a long time to come if Summer had to guess.

"Is it okay if I call my mom?" Harper asked.

"Of course, it is. Where are you from?" Summer wanted to calm Harper down before she worried her parents.

"San Antonio," Harper said, gripping her phone like it was a grenade.

"Is this your freshman year?"

Harper nodded. Her eyes were still saucers and she was probably still in a little bit of shock.

Lights with sirens filled the air. A patrol car pulled up alongside the curb. An officer got out and within a few minutes, Thick Guy was seated in the back of a squad car. The officer took statements, and then thanked them.

Dawson introduced himself to Harper once the dust had settled.

"I said we'd take her home," Summer said.

There was no hesitation in Dawson's voice as he agreed. Within twenty minutes, he reached the address on campus and deposited Harper at her dorm.

He returned to the truck and asked, "How are you doing with all this?"

"Fine. It's crazy to run into him."

"I'm sure as hell glad we did. He invoked his right to remain silent," Dawson said as he navigated them back onto the freeway that, even at this time of night, was stacked with vehicles.

"He's obviously been in this situation before."

"Wouldn't surprise me if he had a rap sheet longer than my arm," Dawson admitted.

"The officer said he'd see us at the station. Does that mean we're headed there now?" she asked.

"No. He won't talk and there's nothing we can do about it. You already gave your statement. We'll swing by tomorrow morning when the detective who worked Cheryl's case is in. I have a few questions I'd like to ask her."

"You don't like how she handled the investigation, do you?" It wasn't really a question.

"Not really. I think she tried to pin the whole thing on Yarnell. He was a little too easy to try to nail. But the guy didn't do it. An experienced detective would've seen it right away. I'd like to know what I'm dealing with when it comes to Detective Libby and that's best done in a face-to-face meeting."

Despite cars as far as she could see on either side of her, in front of her and behind her, they were still moving. The progress was slow but she'd take it.

Forty minutes later in a drive that should've taken fifteen, Dawson pulled in front of the hotel and then around to the side of the building to park.

"I hope Harper called her mom." It was a strange thought to have now. Summer wondered what is was like to have that. She'd known that her mother had loved her children in her own way. She'd just been so broken that she kept herself too medicated to show it.

If Summer ever became a mother, she'd be the kind a child wanted to call in an emergency. Someone a child could lean on during tough times. She'd want to be part of her child's life like she imagined Dawson would be. His entire family was a support system for each other. What was that even like?

If she had a child, and she'd never really given it much thought, she'd want to have one with a man like Dawson. He'd be an amazing father.

Summer gave herself a mental slap to root herself back in reality.

Where did all that come from? She'd never once thought about what it would be like to have children. Now she couldn't help but wonder if it was because she'd never been around a man she trusted enough to try.

DAWSON WALKED SIDE by side with Summer through the hotel lobby. At this hour, there were very few folks downstairs. The only group he saw was a family of four with their luggage being wheeled to the check-in desk.

He and Summer made it to the room without anyone giving them a second look.

"Do you think it's an odd coincidence that the guy who was after me was in Drake Yarnell's neighborhood?" she asked.

"His name is Jesse Lynch." Dawson couldn't say he was surprised. "It's one of the worst neighborhoods in Austin. We got lucky running into Lynch when we did but I can't say I'm surprised we saw him in that general area."

"Do you think he was behind the murders?" she asked.

"Not Lynch. I do believe he's for hire and someone used him to get to your sister and possibly Cheryl. A violin string might be his MO."

"Autumn and Cheryl didn't know each other as far as we can tell." Summer kicked off her shoes and reclaimed her seat on the sofa.

Dawson joined her, opening the laptop and entering the password to bring the screen to life.

"They were connected by the killer," she continued. "That's obvious. But it was someone they'd both dated."

"There's the coffee shop," he added.

"I can't help but think we need to park it there tomorrow and watch everyone who comes through those doors." The lines in Summer's forehead deepened as she concentrated. Her lips pursed and her unfocused gaze stared at the screen even though she wasn't really looking at it. "If he walks in, he's bound to have some kind of reaction to seeing me alive."

"It will also alert him to the fact you exist. Your sister seemed to go to great lengths to keep you hidden and I'm certain it was for good reason."

"What about the necklace, though?" she asked.

"She had to know you'd go through her stuff eventually even if it was just to toss it in the trash."

"It's possible she wanted me to figure out the connection with you." It was all speculation but that was all they had at the moment.

"What about Sean Menendez?" she asked.

"We can stop by the apartment complex on our way in town," he said. He also made a mental note to check with Detective Libby about the name Matt Shank, the fake lawyer name that Autumn had put on the divorce papers.

Summer glanced at the clock on the wall and bit back a yawn. "What time do you want to head downtown tomorrow?"

"We could get a jump on traffic. Say, six o'clock in the morning. If the apartment complex doesn't net any leads we could stop for breakfast before heading to the station." He wanted to stay up and peruse the files to get a better handle on all the statements and evidence.

Summer excused herself to the bathroom, returning twenty minutes later wearing a hotel bathrobe. She had the waist cinched up tightly. She stopped at the doorway to the bedroom. She bit her bottom lip and shifted her weight from side to side. Was she nervous?

"Will you lie down with me until I fall asleep?" she asked. "Every time I close my eyes, I see those pictures in my head." She motioned toward the laptop and he immediately knew she was talking about Cheryl.

"Yeah, sure." He said the words casually like lying down next to Summer in bed would be no big deal. His pulse kicked up thinking about being in such close proximity to her. Since he no longer ran on hormones and caffeine like in his younger days, he told himself he could handle it. And he could. There was no way he'd cross a boundary with Summer that she didn't want.

The problem was that when he stood up, he saw desire in her eyes. Desire for comfort. Desire to get lost in someone. Desire to shut out the world for just a few hours.

Dawson took her by the hand and linked their fingers, ignoring all the electrical impulses firing through him as best he could. It wasn't easy. Being this close to Summer wasn't easy. But the easy road was underrated.

He lifted the covers for her, and she climbed into bed. He knew better than to follow, so he toed off his boots and propped up a couple of pillows. He sat on top of the comforter and even then his heart detonated when she curled her body around his.

Dawson watched as she fell into a deep sleep beside him. He closed his eyes, telling himself a catnap would do him some good.

The next sound he heard was the snick of a lock.

Chapter Sixteen

"Housekeeping." The small voice along with a knock on the door caused Dawson to shoot straight up to standing.

The sun was already up and he realized he'd fallen asleep. He couldn't remember the last time that had happened when he'd intended to stay awake. He missed the feel of Summer's warm body the minute he stood up.

A cursory look said he hadn't peeled his shirt off in the middle of the night and his jeans were still snapped. He was decent enough to face the person coming into their room. He cursed himself for not putting the Do Not Disturb sign on the door handle.

He moved to the doorway, trying not to wake Summer as he glanced at the clock. Seven a.m.

"Sorry," he said to the short, middle-aged woman standing at the door. She couldn't be much taller than five feet. "My wife is still asleep. Do you mind coming back in about an hour?"

"No problem, sir." The round woman with the

graying hair and kind eyes waved as she took a backward step in the opened door. "I'll come back."

"Thank you." Dawson followed her to the door and put the sign out. When he returned, Summer was sitting up and rubbing her eyes. Seeing that honey-wheat hair spill down the pillow he'd been sleeping on moments ago didn't do good things to his heart this early. He made a beeline for the coffee machine and raked his hand through his hair.

As the coffee brewed in his cup, he made a quick pit stop to the bathroom to wash his face and brush his teeth. Splashing cold water on his face helped shake him out of the fog that had him going down a path of real feelings for Summer.

She was in trouble and he was helping her out. That was all. She needed answers to what happened to her sister. That was all. He was going to nail the bastard who killed Autumn and then walk away from the Grayson family. That was all.

Too bad his mantra wasn't working. There were so many cracks in the casing around his heart there was no threat he'd use it instead of his Kevlar vest for protection.

As he exited the bathroom, Summer stood on the other side of the door. She squeezed past him as soon as he opened it.

"Coffee?" he asked.

"Yes, please." The door closed and he heard the water running as he moved into the next room. He didn't need to stick around the door and think about the fact she was naked underneath that robe any more than he needed the image of her waking up next to him etched in his brain.

Because it felt more right than anything had in longer than he cared to remember.

A couple of sips of fresh brew should shake his brain out of the fog and keep it on track. He brought both cups over to the coffee table and retrieved his cell phone. He called the station and identified himself. He was immediately transferred to a supervisor, which he'd expected.

"This is Sergeant Wexler. How may I be of assistance?" Wexler had one of those voices that made him sound like he'd been on the job longer than he cared to and had seen just about everything. He was the two *C*s: curt and courteous.

"My name is Marshal O'Connor and I'm calling to check on a suspect by the name of Jesse Lynch."

"Right." There was an ominous quality to Wexler's tone. "I'm sorry to be the one to tell you but Lynch hung himself last night."

This news was the first indication this case was bigger than Dawson realized. He'd been thinking the perp was someone small-time who'd dated Cheryl and then Autumn. He got a taste of what it was like to kill with Cheryl. It had possibly even been an accident or an argument that had gone too far. By the time he got to Autumn, he'd developed a taste for it. The guy was someone who had access to a violin string, an unlikely murder weapon. A musician or music teacher? It also made a statement because strangulation was a very personal method for murder.

"I'm sorry to hear the news." Dawson had no doubt in his mind that Jesse Lynch was not the type to hang himself in his cell, especially considering they'd caught him before he'd done anything to the young coed. The case against him wouldn't stick if he had a decent lawyer.

Summer was a different story altogether. But then all he'd done was chase her. He hadn't actually caught her. All the evidence against him was hearsay.

"It's a shame," Wexler said in a tsk-tsk tone. "Young people today have a lot of emotional problems. A university kid was sitting on the side of the road the other day with a flat tire. He was bawling and pacing. I calmed him down and told him I'd help him. I was tired. On my way home from a long day but if it was my kid, I'd want someone to stop. So, I'm working on the tire and he stops crying but instead of jumping in to help, do you know what he does?"

Wexler paused.

"Can't say that I do," Dawson supplied.

"He gets on his cell and starts snap-ticking a friend…or whatever that social media site is. The one where the kids send messages to their friends instead of calling."

Dawson wished Wexler would get to the point.

"I had to tell him, no-no. Get the hell off that thing and get over here. You're going to learn how to change a tire." He finished his sentence in ta-da fashion.

"Next time he'll know how to do it himself." Dawson had no idea how to respond or how this story was linked to Jesse Lynch's hanging.

"Yeah, that's what I was thinking. I can do it for him and he'll never learn or I can tell him to put the damn phone away and pay attention. These kids are lazy and the minute anything goes wrong, they fall apart." Wexler might believe that about Jesse Lynch but Dawson didn't.

Based on what he knew so far, Lynch was street-smart. He got by working the streets and taking what he wanted. He was from the wrong side of the tracks though. Not a kid who got busted for a dime bag of weed and thought his parents would never speak to him again.

This kid knew how to survive.

"Was he alone in his cell all night?" Dawson asked.

"According to the night watch, he was."

Dawson didn't like the sound of that. It could mean the killer was someone on the inside or had connections. The violin string bothered him, though.

"Thank you for letting me know about Lynch. That's unfortunate," Dawson said.

"Such a waste," Wexler said.

"Can you do me a favor?" Dawson asked.

"Sure, anything."

"Transfer me to Detective Libby." The quiet on the line sent another warning flare.

"She isn't around."

Dawson wasn't so sure what that meant but it sounded like a sore subject.

"When will she be back?" he asked.

"She's not with the department anymore," Wexler supplied.

"What happened?" Dawson asked.

"She left the department about two years ago."

"Do you have a forwarding address?"

"I can transfer you to personnel," Wexler offered.

Now Dawson needed to decide if the sergeant was involved or just complacent. His instincts said the latter was true.

"I'll call back another time." Dawson wanted to give the impression he didn't care all that much, so he added, "It's not that important."

Wexler seemed satisfied with that answer. "You take care."

"Will do." He ended the call. When he glanced up, he saw Summer studying him.

"What happened to Jesse Lynch?" Her forehead was creased with concern that their first lead had just dried up.

"He was murdered in his cell last night, but the department is calling it a suicide."

Stunned, Summer took a couple of steps backward until she sat in a chair at the small table. She seemed to pick up on the implication.

"I checked all the names of the politicians in Austin and didn't find a single Charles, Charlie, Charley or Matthew and no relation to the last name of Shank." Dawson reviewed his findings or lack thereof with her.

"So, Lynch is gone." She paused like she needed a minute for the news to sink in. Like saying it out loud made it that much more real and scary. "What about the detective on the case?"

"She quit the department six months after Cheryl's murder." The timing of her resignation was suspect as hell. The whole situation reeked of foul play.

"And this is the same department that is going to investigate my sister's murder?" Summer brought her hand up to her face.

"They gave Cheryl's case to a young detective. I'm guessing they didn't expect her to do a very good job being so green," he stated.

"Except that she stayed with it. We thought she was pulled off the case and it was marked cold, when it turns out she left the department. What would make her do that?"

"I'll ask Colton to look into it and see if he can dig up some information. He has a trusted contact at Austin PD and that might be our best route. I can call human resources but they won't be able to give out personal information about the detective." Her exit must have been the reason the investigation stalled.

"What would make her up and leave like that?"

"Bribery. Threats. Your guess is as good as mine. If we can figure out where she landed after leaving and how she's living now, we'll have a better idea of the reason."

And just who the department was trying to protect.

THIS NEWS WAS BIG. It screamed cover-up. And if the same person killed Autumn, there'd be no justice for her. If the person was so big or connected that he could make a detective leave her job and a witness be killed in jail and marked as a suicide, how could they bring him down? Who would listen?

"I got away," she said under her breath. "He must've had eyes on the jail in case one of his minions got picked up."

"Or Lynch used his one phone call to the wrong person."

"Why not just kill him before?" she asked.

"He wasn't done with the job, for one. Plus, the body count was racking up."

"There were two guys chasing me." She wondered what had happened to the second one.

"It's possible he's still out there. Once word gets out in their circles that Lynch is dead, the others will likely go underground for a few months. Maybe even hop over the border." He referred to Mexico. "There are plenty of little towns to get lost in."

She'd read about Americans living in both countries. It was easy to move back and forth with US citizenship. She'd also read about young people going over to party and never coming back. Many border towns were dangerous. But then, Scrappy wasn't exactly a college coed and he wasn't exactly innocent.

"I doubt Sean Menendez has the kind of connections necessary to pull off a jail murder." Dawson was right about that.

"Agreed." She didn't care how creepy the maintenance man was, he'd be hard-pressed to find the resources it took to kill someone while in a jail cell.

"Do you think we can stop by and talk to him or the property manager anyway? Maybe I can get some information about my sister from the staff."

"It doesn't hurt to stop by for an interview. I also need to let my brother know what's going on." Dawson paused and stared at his phone. "No one at Austin P.D. knew your sister had been murdered."

"The coroner must be honest," she observed.

"I've known him a long time. He's always been one of the good guys."

"If you ever needed proof the coroner reported the death but it was covered up by Austin P.D, I think you just got it." She picked up her coffee cup and took a sip. The burn felt good on her throat. "You said Yarnell has been living in hell ever since Cheryl's murder. I can't imagine what he must've gone through with a department bent on hanging a crime on him."

"The guy was in pain learning about his ex. She'd tried to call him and his new girlfriend picked up. She said a few choice words to Cheryl and that was it. She never tried to contact him again and then she shows up dead." Dawson studied his cell phone screen. It started going off in his hand like crazy.

He immediately stood up and started pacing. A feeling deep in the pit of her stomach caused her to be nauseous because the look on his face said it was bad news—news about his beloved family.

"Sorry, I need to—"

"Don't apologize, Dawson. Your family is just as important as mine."

He stopped and looked at her, a bit shell-shocked. And then he nodded, smiled and made a call.

Summer was confused by his look of surprise. His family was important to him, and to her. He was becoming important to her. There was something about living in fear of her life for the past few weeks that made the grand scheme of things crystal clear. Family came first.

And maybe clarity had to do with the fact that she'd lost hers. Summer had always believed in family. She'd just never really had more than her sister.

She couldn't help but overhear Dawson's conversation despite the fact he'd gone into the bedroom for privacy. There was news about his father's case. An address came up for a possible suspect.

Dawson ended the call before walking into the room, a look of despair darkened his eyes.

"I overheard bits and pieces of your conversation. I'm sorry—"

He shook his head before raking a finger through his thick curls. A couple laps around the room later, and he seemed to calm down enough to tell her what was going on.

"Do you need to go investigate?" She didn't expect Dawson to stay with her under the circumstances.

"One extra person would just be in the way. My brothers are all over it and I'm needed here." The look on his face said he wanted to be with his siblings.

"You don't have to do this, Dawson. Your family needs you and I wouldn't want you to have any regrets about—"

He wheeled around on her so fast, she stopped midsentence.

"Last time I checked, you were family, too." His voice was sharp, and his eyes shot daggers. "But if you don't want me here then say the word."

Her entire body stiffened as she geared up for a fight. Before she could open her mouth to argue Dawson shot her a look of apology. He put a hand up and took another couple of laps.

Summer drew in a few breaths meant to calm her but all she ended up doing was breathing in more of his spicy and clean scent. She tried to form words but none came.

All she wanted was to stand up and put her hand on his chest to stop him and get him to breathe. So, that's exactly what she did. Summer stood up and then stepped in front of him, forcing him to stop. Hand to his chest, she locked gazes with him.

He started to speak and clamped down, compressing his lips instead.

She could feel the moment the air changed from anger and frustration to awareness. Awareness of their hearts pounding against their rib cages. Awareness of the chemistry that had been sizzling between them since the moment they'd met. Awareness of their raspy breathing.

Call her wrong, but one look in his eyes made her think he wanted to reach out to her as much as she needed to feel him. She ran her fingers along the muscled ridges of his chest. There was only a thin layer of cotton preventing her from skin-to-skin contact.

Dawson brought his hands up to cup her face. He looked at her with a longing so deep it robbed her breath.

The need to feel his lips move against hers was a physical ache. She tilted her face toward his and he brought his lips down on hers.

Summer brought her hands up to his shoulders to brace herself, digging her nails in when he deepened the kiss. His hands dropped and his arms looped around her waist, bringing her body flush with his. She could kiss this man all day. She *wanted* to kiss this man all day.

She couldn't.

Reality lurked and they'd come to their senses in a minute. But for right then, Summer didn't care about his past or hers. Nothing mattered except this moment happening between them, a moment they both wanted so badly they could hardly breathe.

She felt that kiss from her crown to her toes and when his tongue dipped inside her mouth, heat spread through her. She ignored the fact he was the best kisser in her life and the other obvious fact that he'd be mind-numbingly amazing in bed.

The other facts, she couldn't ignore so easily.

They didn't have a lot of time to waste. Kissing him had been a luxury. And she needed to pull back while she still could.

Easier said than done.

With a deep breath, she managed to break away from those full lips of his—lips too soft for a face of such hard angles.

One look in his eyes said they were playing with fire.

Chapter Seventeen

Dawson pressed his forehead to Summer's while he took a minute to catch his breath. Being with her was doing things to his heart that he never knew possible. Rather than get inside his head about what that meant, how that changed things for him, he re-focused on just breathing with her.

He knew one thing was certain. He'd had great sex in his life before and none of it would compare to what he would have with Summer. He meant that on every level. She had that rare kind of beauty that started on the inside.

Her smile, rare as it might be, was so genuine she radiated. She smiled from her soul, if that made any sense. Hell, he'd never been the poetic type, but she made him want to put his attraction to her into words. He just needed to find the right ones first.

There hadn't been much to laugh about lately but when she did he could swear it was the most beautiful sound. There wasn't a musical instrument in existence that compared to her, and hearing it did things to his heart that he'd tried to shut down long ago. It made him think of foreign things like forever—something he'd thought would never be possible after the way his marriage ended.

He'd cared about Autumn and had been determined to make things work because of the child he thought she was carrying. There was no forcing his feelings when it came to Summer.

Her face was blue skies and sunshine after a storm. Her mind kept him on his toes. And the fire burning inside her made him think life with her would never be dull.

But that wasn't on the table. He wasn't sure he could go down that road again with anyone. If he did…he'd want it to be with Summer.

After feathering a kiss to her lips, he cleared his throat and took a step back, hoping for a little clarity. Looking into her eyes only muddied the waters for him even more.

Damn.

He needed more coffee to wake him up because he wasn't thinking clearly. He'd promised himself that he wouldn't let things get out of hand with Summer and he had every intention of keeping that commitment to himself.

Besides, with his personal life in upheaval, this was the worst possible time to add more confusion into the mix. Summer didn't deserve that, either. She needed a strong shoulder to lean on while she got her bearings. The woman was fully capable of handling herself and yet he wanted to be her comfort in a storm.

Best not to confuse the sentiment with emotions. He'd keep himself in check better than he had been. For Summer's sake.

THE APARTMENT COMPLEX downtown wasn't exactly the kind Summer could see her sister living in. It was most likely what she could afford, and that broke Summer's heart even more. Why hadn't Autumn reached out for help? Why did she live like this? Was this place better than being with Summer?

She reached inside her purse where she kept the "Summer" necklace and rolled it around in her fingers. In a strange way, touching this piece of junk jewelry made her feel more connected to a sister who she admittedly didn't know very well.

This was the last place she would've looked for Autumn. Maybe that was part of the reason her sister rented an apartment here.

Dawson parked the truck and they both got out. The office was a small brick building with double glass doors. The sign said it was open. She took a deep breath and started toward the entrance.

For the life of her she couldn't figure out why her sister would've left twenty-five thousand dollars sitting in a bank account in her name without touching it. The money had been a gift from Dawson. It was free and clear with no expectation of payback.

Had Autumn regretted getting him involved in her life? Had she walked away and tried to minimize the damage?

If she didn't take anything from him, did she

think she could convince herself the lies she'd told him were for his protection? It was possible she convinced herself that her disappearing act was harmless.

Did she leave Dawson to go back to the secret boyfriend she'd been involved with in the past? All signs pointed to just that. She remembered what Dawson said about women in abusive relationships. She just wished she'd known what her sister was going through. She could've been there for Autumn. Her sister wasn't alone.

A rogue tear escaped thinking about Autumn.

Summer wiped it away and stepped inside the glass doors. A little bell rang when Dawson opened the one on the right. Inside there was a tiled foyer. Beyond that was a great room overlooking a small pool. There was a kitchenette and two offices.

An overeager youngish woman dressed in a pantsuit bounded into the room. She had Shirley Temple curls and wore too much makeup to pull off the innocent look.

"Hello, I'm Marcy." She stuck out her hand toward Dawson.

Her gaze lingered a little too long on his face and Summer wanted to snap her fingers at the woman to get her attention.

"Dawson, and this is my wife—"

"Sandy." She nodded like she'd just answered the last question correctly on a game show. "I know."

Summer reined in her confused look because she realized this person might know her sister.

"I just didn't realize you were married." Marcy had one of those voices that grated. Fingernails on a chalkboard sounded like a relief after hearing her speak.

"Oh, right. I forgot to mention it because we've been separated. You know, trying to figure things out."

Marcy looked from Dawson to Summer and laughed. "You've been busy."

She flexed and released her fingers as she felt Dawson's hand clasp hers. He gave a little squeeze and it grounded her. They had a purpose and the ever-annoying Marcy didn't get to detract from that. Besides, she didn't seem very bright, which was a potential gold mine of information for them if they played it right.

"Your things have been boxed up. Headquarters makes us hold on to them for ninety days after eviction." Marcy shrugged.

"Oh. Right. I guess I forgot to keep my rent payments up once I got back together with my husband," Summer said by way of explanation, ignoring the fact that calling Dawson her husband had just rolled right off her tongue like it was truth. Not being honest hit her at her core but couldn't be helped if she wanted access to Autumn's things.

"I almost didn't recognize you at first. You look so…different." Marcy made a show of looking Summer up and down.

"Well, it's me." She had to tamp down the urge to come back with a snarky remark. This wasn't the right time for pride. "Is it possible to see my belongings?"

Marcy blew out a sharp breath and gave Summer a death stare.

"It's against policy when there's an overdue rent situation," she huffed, making her disgust with anyone who was late on rent clear as if the glaring eyes hadn't done it already.

"Do you take a credit card?" Dawson stepped up immediately. "I didn't bring a check with me today."

The annoying woman perked up at the sound of payment.

"We add 3 percent to the outstanding balance," she warned like that might be a tipping point that caused them to turn around and walk out the door.

Summer almost laughed out loud. Dawson O'Connor could cover 3 percent and so much more. He could keep the twenty-five thousand dollars in Autumn's bank account, and Summer would figure out a payment plan to cover her sister's expenses.

"Just give me a total." Dawson smiled and Marcy practically beamed back at him. It was enough to make Summer hold his hand a little tighter. And, yes, she was being territorial.

Dawson's smile was meant to disarm Marcy. Summer figured that part out on her own and yet a streak of jealousy still crept in. Keeping a safe distance from her emotions had always been a matter of survival for Summer.

Despite the magnetic pull toward Dawson and the absolute fire in every kiss that promised so much more than great sex, breaking down her walls would take time and patience. She didn't even know if it was possible anymore. In every past relationship she'd been afraid of heights and there'd been a cliff in the distance.

Before Dawson, she wouldn't consider getting anywhere near the edge. Now? She was starting to think that maybe it could happen. The problem wasn't the relationship. She knew being with a person as intelligent, kind and respectful as Dawson would set the bar for every future date. When the shine wore off and it ended, she would be shattered.

Because she wouldn't be able to keep Dawson at a distance. He was the sun, drawing everything that got near into his orbit, spinning faster and making her forget that if she stepped out, she'd spiral out of control.

"Let me check with my property manager," Marcy chirped. Suddenly, fingernails on a chalkboard didn't seem so bad to Summer.

Dawson thanked her before tugging Summer a little bit closer and dipping his head to press a kiss on her lips.

Marcy exited quickly and it made Summer smirk. The move from Dawson was most likely meant to sell the marriage story but damned if it didn't feel like the most natural thing for him to kiss her. Summer was in his orbit all right. Pulling away from him when this came to a close might be more difficult than she'd anticipated.

Still, walking away would be the right thing to

do, she reasoned. There was no other choice when she really thought about it. This case would end. She needed to get used to a new normal and a life without Autumn. Her sister had been preparing Summer for this in many ways over the past few years.

Autumn had been difficult to get ahold of and she'd disappeared for long periods. She'd been putting more and more emotional distance between them. The notion of looking through her sister's last possessions hit her so hard it nearly knocked her breath away. So many thoughts raced through Summer's mind about what her sister had held on to. How had her sister lived in those final months? What had been important to her?

Irritating chirp lady walked back into the lobby.

"You owe three months' rent at one thousand five hundred and fifty dollars a month. Plus, four hundred and fifty dollars in late fees and a thousand dollars for us to release your belongings. The total comes to six thousand, one hundred dollars." She produced an invoice.

Dawson pulled his wallet out of his back pocket. "Do you have a preference when it comes to plastic?"

"We'll take whatever you have available as long as the charge is approved." Marcy beamed at Dawson but when her gaze shifted to Summer, her forehead creased with disapproval.

He didn't hesitate to hand over his card.

"I'll be right back as soon as I run this," Marcy said before bebopping out of the room.

"I'd like to pay you back," Summer said in a whisper.

"You don't have to worry about that. It's the least I can do," he said and there was regret in his voice.

"What do you mean?" she asked.

"I let your sister down. She came to me for sanctuary and I couldn't protect her." His serious tone said he meant every word. Here, Summer had been so focused on the fact she'd let her sister down she hadn't once stopped to think Dawson might be in the same boat.

"You didn't know her. She walked out. You believed her. You did nothing but trust her and she betrayed that. Don't get me wrong, I love Autumn with all my heart. That doesn't mean I'm naive to the fact she made a lot of bad decisions in her life. But believe me when I say that you're the last person on earth who should feel responsible for her."

"Your card is good," Marcy interrupted the conversation.

Logic said Summer should be able to forgive herself for not being there when Autumn needed her. The advice she'd given to Dawson seconds ago was true for him and somewhere down deep she could acknowledge it was true for her, too.

Dawson took the card Marcy held between them. He tucked it back inside his wallet at the same time Marcy seemed to catch sight of the badge. She looked up at Dawson and studied his face.

Summer couldn't tell what the woman was thinking but the badge seemed to make her stand up a little straighter.

"Where do you keep eviction belongings?" Dawson asked. It was the question on Summer's mind.

"You'll have to wait thirty days and then you can buy them back from us." Marcy sounded a little less certain of herself and a lot less bubbly than she had a few minutes ago.

"We paid up my rent with late fees plus the thousand dollars to release those belongings. There's no reason to keep my stuff." Summer tensed up, ready for a fight.

Dawson squeezed her hand.

"How much to buy all of her belongings?" he asked.

Marcy glanced around. "I'm not really supposed to—"

"I don't trust that you've taken care of my stuff. I'd like to check on it to make sure everything's there." Summer was grasping at straws here but there might be something in her sister's personal items that could give a hint of who she'd been seeing. Leaving empty-handed wasn't an option.

"We have the right to dispose of your items. We sent out a notice of our intentions—"

"Which technically I never received."

"Your…" Marcy's gaze bounced from Summer to Dawson and back "…*boyfriend* stopped by a couple of months ago and emptied out your storage. There isn't much left but some makeup and toiletries. There are a few towels and some clothing. I don't think my boss would be too mad if I showed you what was left."

The wheels were already turning in Summer's mind as to how to tactfully ask what her "boyfriend" looked like.

"That would be great if it's not too much trouble." Summer softened her tone, reminding herself she'd get more out of Marcy with honey than vinegar.

"Stay right here and I'll get my keys." Marcy disappeared long enough for Summer to make eyes at Dawson.

He seemed to read her apprehension even though he didn't speak. How had he become so important in such a short time? She'd tell herself the desperate life-and-death situation she'd been in would cause her emotions to be all over the place. But that wouldn't be fair to her feelings for Dawson.

Marcy returned and motioned for them to follow her. She led them to a golf cart parked out front. Summer climbed inside and looked around. The person who'd killed her sister had walked around on these same paths. Cheryl's killer had been here.

No way to bring up Summer's "boyfriend" came to her tactfully. So, Summer took the front seat and leaned over when Marcy claimed the driver's side and popped the key in the ignition.

"I don't want my husband to hear this but can you tell me which one of my boyfriends stopped by. I dated around a lot after my husband and I separated. We got married straight out of high school and needed to find ourselves as people." She was overexplaining, adding details to convince Marcy of the untruth.

Marcy mouthed an *Oh*.

The woman winked and smiled, looking a little too happy that "Sandy" seemed to be a little loose.

Chapter Eighteen

"He introduced himself as Matt...um, hmm. That's weird. I'm not sure he ever told me his last name. If he did, I sure don't remember it. He was gorgeous, though." She glanced back at Dawson, who was making a show of checking his cell phone.

Luckily, the backseat faced the opposite direction so they couldn't see his face. It gave the illusion he couldn't hear.

Marcy backed out of the parking spot. The beep, beep, beep of the golf cart masked their conversation.

"If you ask me, this one's the best. Hands down." Marcy blushed as she nodded back toward Dawson. "But then I've always been partial to tall, muscled men. Matt looked like he stepped out of one of those Abercrombie and Fitch ads if there was one for middle-aged men. You know?"

"Yeah." Summer didn't have a clue. She'd gotten a first name, though. Matt. The name of the so-called attorney who'd handled the fake divorce had been Matt Charley Shank. The first two names were clues. What did Shank mean?

For some reason, Summer doubted it was his actual last name. In fact, she was certain that Dawson would have checked every Matt or Matthew Shank in Texas. She tabled that thought, figuring Marcy was feeling chatty.

"I never liked his hair, though," Summer said.

"Too curly?"

"Exactly. And the color—"

"Black never bothered me. It was a little long for a guy who wore a suit, though," Marcy stated.

Summer committed the details to memory. Matt, last name unknown, who looked like he'd walked off an Abercrombie and Fitch ad for middle-aged men, had curly black hair.

"His eyes were nice, though," Marcy continued in a hushed tone as she whipped around a corner and toward the back side of the complex. They passed a row of mailboxes before Marcy made another turn. "I don't normally like blue eyes on a man but his were so light. They looked good on him. And he had just enough gray at the temples to be sexy."

She added the extra details, repeating his description to seal it into her brain. Matt, last name unknown, who looked like he'd walked off an Abercrombie and Fitch ad for middle-aged men, had curly black hair. He also had light blue eyes and wore a suit. And he had just enough gray at the temples to be sexy.

A picture was emerging.

"He turned out to be a creep." Summer fished for any signs there'd been fighting between her sister and Matt. Marcy seemed like the nosy type who would know if a couple had problems.

"Really?" Marcy seemed shocked. She took a minute to think about it and then said, "You know, that explains all the flowers."

"His way of apologizing," Summer continued.

"My mom always said never trust a man when he sends flowers out of the blue. It means he's doing something wrong." Marcy looked at Summer in a show of solidarity.

Summer noticed there was no ring on Marcy's left hand.

"Dating is hard," Summer continued.

"It's the worst." Marcy smacked her palm on the steering wheel. "Right?"

"There are so many jerks out there," Summer agreed.

"And they take all shapes and forms." Marcy was really into the conversation now. Good, Summer had gotten good information out of the woman so far. And Summer was getting used to her nasal tone of voice. Fingernails on a chalkboard still had a better sound but Marcy was growing on her.

Summer repeated her new mantra. Matt, last name unknown, who looked like he'd walked off an Abercrombie and Fitch ad for middle-aged men, had curly black hair that was a little too long. He also had light blue eyes and wore a suit. And he had just enough gray at the temples to be sexy.

"You think you can trust a guy in a suit and then he turns out to be more of a jerk than you could ever have imagined." Summer kept pouring it on. She was always so careful when she met a new person and was always guarded if someone tried to interact with her for the first time online. She'd been too busy working extra shifts and socking away money to have much free time. When she did have a day off, she usually spent it at the library researching how to start her own business or under the covers trying to catch up on her sleep.

Marcy rocked her head as she pulled into a parking spot. Dawson, who'd been quiet up until now, was off the cart first. He clasped hands with Summer the second she exited.

"Right this way." Marcy took them to a storage building with five large doors. Keys clanked as she searched for the right one. "Hold on just a minute. Where'd you go?" She was talking to herself as she checked keys, one by one, and occasionally glanced over at Summer with an awkward smile.

At least Marcy was focusing on Summer now instead of Dawson. He moved behind Summer and looped his arms around her. The feel of his masculine chest against her back sent sensual shivers racing through her.

In the move, he also slipped his cell phone into her hands and swiped so that the screen came to life.

"Are you from Texas, Marcy?"

Summer could feel his chest vibrate when he spoke. More of those inappropriate shivers raced down her back.

"San Angelo originally." She beamed at him before refocusing on the keys. She slid one in and said, "Finally."

When her back was turned, Summer glanced at the screen of Dawson's phone. He'd written down the description of Matt, which was basically the same as the mantra she'd repeated a couple of times since getting off the cart.

He ran his thumb inside the palm of her hand, and it sent a trail of warmth.

"And, we're in," Marcy said after wrestling with the door. "Be careful. We don't usually let people back here, so it's a mess. Maintenance is supposed to clean up but Jared has been calling in sick lately and it's all we can do to keep residents happy."

"What happened to Sean?" Summer took the opportunity to ask another question that had been on both her and Dawson's minds.

"We had to let him go," Marcy said with a frown. "He made a few of our female residents uncomfortable, so he wasn't working out." She paused. "I didn't realize you liked him all that much."

"Can't say that I knew him very well." She shrugged. "Now that you mention it, he was a little creepy."

"That's the same word a few other residents used to describe interactions with him," she admitted. Those few minutes in the golf cart had won over Marcy's trust.

Steeling her nerves, Summer followed Marcy into the space. She flipped on a light, which was one of those basic builder installs hanging from the ceiling.

The walls inside weren't finished. There were only boards and posts.

The storage shed was large and there was enough dust on the flooring to cover half the state. People's belongings were stacked in piles, some were wrapped in what looked like oversize pieces of Saran wrap.

Marcy navigated around a few of the piles until she located Autumn's belongings.

"Here's your stuff," she said to Summer.

The stack consisted of a pile of clothing on top of shoes. There was makeup, like Marcy had mentioned before. There wasn't a whole lot else. A couple of purses, some blankets and toiletries.

"I'll go get the truck," Dawson said as an icy chill raced down Summer's spine. All of her sister's belongings could easily fit in the back.

Summer didn't have much, but she'd worked for her small apartment and filled it with things she loved. Her neighbor was looking after Summer's plants. She had a wall of bookshelves with her favorite paperbacks. There were a few shells from the beach along with art she'd bought on the street. She'd made a few pieces herself, nothing fancy, just pottery she'd painted and fired. She had the most comfortable bed and her blanket was the softest thing she'd ever felt.

Again, nothing extravagant but everything in her home meant something to her. She still had a white starfish blown from glass that she'd picked up in Seattle at the Pike Place Market. Clothes weren't her big thing and neither were purses and shoes. She carried a handbag, of course, but back home she usually just stuck her wallet inside her backpack and moved on. It was easier to carry and keep track of that way.

Nothing really stood out in her sister's personal effects but she wanted to take them home with her anyway. This was all she had left of Autumn.

She glanced up in time to see Marcy studying her.

"If you don't mind my saying so, I like the natural look on you much better than what you did before."

"I'll take all the compliments I can get." Summer realized if there was anything important, Matt would have picked it up when he came and got Autumn's stuff. He must've been worried something might link her back to him.

"Don't take it the wrong way. You were always beautiful, but you never really talked much."

"I was going through a lot while deciding if we were going to give our marriage another shot." Summer felt defensive of her sister, which was silly. Marcy didn't mean anything by it and she didn't come across as the most sensitive person.

"There are earrings in the makeup holder that I had my eye on to buy," she admitted and then seemed to catch herself. "Before I realized you were coming back for your stuff, of course. Most people never do. Once they skip out on rent, we don't see them again. Their stuff ends up in here and we eventually sell it. My boss takes forever to get rid of this stuff."

All Summer could figure was that was Marcy's way of offering an apology.

"Which earrings did you like?" Summer knelt

down beside the makeup container and then opened it, kicking up a small storm of dust.

Summer coughed.

"Sorry about the dust. No one has run a broom through here in forever." Marcy waved her hand in front of her wrinkled nose.

The makeup container had pockets like a tackle box. Summer unfolded it and in the bottom were several pairs of earrings.

"Those are beautiful." Marcy pointed to an art deco throwback. The pair she was talking about were like chandeliers. They had more sparkle than a craft store's glitter aisle.

Summer picked them up, figuring she could buy a little more good will. "They're yours if you want them."

"Are you serious right now?" Marcy was ecstatic. If a pair of cheap free earrings could do that for her, so be it.

"Definitely." Summer picked them up and held them out.

"I'm not sure I should. I mean, I want to...but... I don't know what the company policy is."

"How about this? They belong to me. I don't want them anymore since I wore them on a date with my ex-boyfriend. I don't think my husband would appreciate me bringing them into our home and I don't want the reminder of a horrible relationship. So, you'd be doing me a favor if you took them off my hands." Summer could tell she was winning Marcy over with her logic.

"Well, if I was doing you a favor…"

"You would be." Summer meant it, too. They were not her style one bit and she'd rather they bring someone else joy than end up at a garage sale. She wouldn't even begin to know what to charge for them.

Marcy took the offering and splayed them out on her flat palm. "They're so gorgeous."

"They'll look better on you than they would on me." Summer caught her slipup, but Marcy was too busy admiring her new earrings to notice.

The door opened and Summer's heart dropped. She stood up a little too fast and scared Marcy.

"Is that you, Dawson?" she asked as she heard boots shuffling across the dusty floor.

"It's me. Pickup is outside. We can gather up your things and head home." He must've noticed the panic in her voice because he was a study in calm when he got to them.

She flashed her eyes at him and he walked straight over to her and kissed her. It was another couple move and probably for show but being with him and especially when he made contact in any way made her feel like she'd found home.

"Truck is backed up as close as I could get it." Dawson realized his mistake in leaving Summer alone the minute he looked into her eyes. He wouldn't do that to her again. He'd jogged back to the front parking lot and gotten back as fast as he could.

A bad feeling caused the hair on the back of his

neck to prick. He'd scoped the area without seeing any cause for alarm and yet that uneasy feeling wouldn't let up.

He was keenly aware that he had Summer at a known hangout of her sister's. The killer was powerful and had connections. He might have eyes everywhere and especially his old haunts.

Dawson was ready to get Summer out of there.

With three of them, loading the truck only took three trips. Marcy had warmed up to Summer, who she believed was Autumn. He noticed Marcy had a pair of earrings tucked into her shirt pocket. They seemed like prize possessions considering she patted her pocket after every load to make sure they didn't fall out somewhere along the way.

When they'd tucked in the last load, he thanked her for her help.

"No problem." She patted her pocket again and looked straight at Summer. "Thank you for these."

Summer smiled one of those genuine, ice-melting smiles that was unique to her at the exact time the crack of a bullet split the air.

Chapter Nineteen

Before Summer had a chance to process what she'd heard, Dawson's arm wrapped around her and he was taking her and Marcy down. He covered them with his heft and the next thing she knew she was on all fours being ushered around the side of the truck.

The sight of blood normally made her sick to her stomach. This time, it sent panic rocketing through her. In the crush of the three of them, she couldn't tell which one of them was bleeding.

Everything started happening fast after that.

"Stay down." Dawson had drawn his weapon and was on his feet in a heartbeat. He made eye contact with Summer. "You got this."

And then he seemed to see the blood, too. He clenched his back teeth and took in a sharp breath.

A bullet whizzed by over his head. In another second, he'd held up his index finger to indicate he'd be right back and then moved toward the driver's side of the truck.

Head low, weapon leading the way, he glanced

over the hood of the truck, fixated on someone and then fired.

Despite originally being from Texas, Summer didn't know much about guns. She couldn't tell what kind Dawson had except that it fired real bullets, one at a time. She scanned her own body looking for signs of a bullet wound but when she looked at Marcy, her stomach sank.

Marcy had that shocked expression that Summer had only seen in movies—a look that said she realized she'd been shot but the news hadn't quite been absorbed yet. Eyes wide, mouth open, she grabbed at her side.

There was a lot of blood. Too much.

Summer jumped into action, sitting on her back haunches and lifting Marcy's blouse on her left hip to assess the damage. The minute she saw the wound area, she knew she needed to stem the bleeding.

She dropped her shoulder, letting her purse fall onto the pavement.

"I need you to do something for me, Marcy," Summer whispered. When that didn't work, she brought her hand up to Marcy's chin and forced her gaze to meet her own. "Find my phone in my purse. I have to put pressure on your wound to stem the bleeding."

Dammit. She wasn't getting through to Marcy.

Oh, well, she didn't have time to waste. She glanced around looking for something she could use. The answer came to her. The scarf. She quickly untied it and then wadded it up into a ball.

"This might hurt but I need you to stay with me, Marcy." Summer had no idea if the woman understood a word, but she had to try to explain. This must be what shock looked like.

The minute Summer put pressure on the wound, Marcy let out a scream and tried to slap away her hand.

"I'm so sorry." Summer had to fight to keep the scarf in place. She took a hard slap to the face. Ringing noises sounded in her ears, but she spun around to her side instead of giving up. She realized Marcy wasn't rational.

With one hand keeping pressure on the wound and the other trying to keep Marcy from digging her fingernails into Summer's shoulder, it was all she could do to contain the situation. And then, out of nowhere, Marcy seemed to snap.

"It's okay," she said.

"Yes. You're going to be okay," Summer confirmed firmly. Marcy needed to hear that Summer believed those words one hundred percent. No question about it. No hesitation.

"Sorry," Marcy said.

There was no time to worry about being polite. Summer didn't fault Marcy one bit for her panic.

"Can you grab my phone out of my purse and call 9-1-1?" Someone in the apartment complex might have already done it by now but Summer had no plans to chance it. She needed to get back up on the way for Dawson.

"Yes. Where?" Marcy glanced around and her eyes landed on the purse. "Oh. Here."

"Just reach in and feel around for it," Summer instructed.

"Got it." Marcy came up with the phone. Her skin was pale but her eyes were bright. She held out the phone. Summer put her thumb on the pad to get through the security feature because it was easier than explaining the step wasn't necessary for emergency calls. The screen came to life and Marcy called for help.

With Marcy's cooperation, Summer could risk a glance toward Dawson. Most of his head and body would be covered by the truck and yet she still panicked that exposed sliver of him could be hit. Realistically, the shooter would have to be an excellent marksman.

He'd missed his mark, Summer. Despite the fact he'd shot Marcy, he clearly wasn't accurate. Summer would have been his target.

Dawson identified himself as a law enforcement officer as Marcy relayed what was happing to the dispatcher on the call.

"Tell them you need an ambulance," Summer urged.

Marcy complied. Now that she'd snapped out of the temporary shock, she seemed to be rational again. Good. They would need all the help they could get.

"She wants to know how bad it is," Marcy said to Summer, glancing down at her wound.

"You're going to be okay. I've stopped the bleeding for now but we're in a situation that could blow up any second. Tell them we don't have any more time."

She did.

"Do they have an ETA?" Summer asked.

Marcy nodded. "An officer is en route. He's five minutes out."

"And the ambulance?" she asked.

"Oh, right." Marcy asked the dispatcher. "Right behind him. They might get here first."

"Okay. We need to get you to a safer spot." Summer glanced around. The storage shed?

No. That wouldn't work. They could be shot while on the move. There was enough furniture inside to hide, though, and it would provide much-needed mass between them and bullets.

Whatever gun this shooter was using seemed to fire one at a time. That was a saving grace that could turn at any second if he had accomplices on the way.

And the storage shed could also trap her and Marcy. What about inside the truck?

It seemed dangerous but offered a getaway.

"Put your hands where I can see them," Dawson commanded.

The response came in the form of a shot being fired.

And then she heard the glorious sound of sirens wailing in the distance. Backup would be there in a matter of minutes.

The sounds of tires squealing from across the parking lot sent an icy chill racing down her spine. The shooter was going to get away.

Dawson hopped into action. He was by her side in a second and pressing a small handgun into the flat of her palm.

"This is the safety and how you take it off. Use the gun if you have to. Go inside the storage shed and find a hiding spot until help arrives." His voice was a study in calm, but his words sent another chill down her back.

Dawson was going after the shooter.

He pressed a kiss to her lips and then he was gone. He climbed into the driver's seat as she helped Marcy to standing.

Summer glanced around as the truck pulled away. Relief washed over her when no one was standing on the opposite side of the parking lot like she'd half feared. The respite was a temporary feeling at best. And it was shattered when she heard another shot ring out.

Marcy flinched.

"We need to tell dispatch where we're going," she said to Marcy, who had a death grip on the cell phone. Within a few seconds, Marcy and Summer were back inside the shed. Marcy mumbled into the phone and, best as Summer could tell, she provided a good update.

At least Marcy knew her way around the storage. Summer flipped off the light and they felt their way around, kicking up enough dust for both of them to cough.

Summer's nose and throat burned but she figured they had more pressing problems at the moment.

DAWSON GUNNED THE ENGINE. He had dispatch on the line. He'd given them a quick rundown of the situation. A uniformed officer was being sent to Summer and Marcy's location along with an ambulance.

He was currently giving chase to a late model SUV, all black with blacked-out windows. The SUV was heading toward the highway where it could get lost in all the traffic. There were temporary plates on the vehicle that, up close, looked like homemade jobs.

The SUV was already onto a road that led to the highway. Dawson cursed under his breath because it had sped up and navigated through enough traffic that he was having difficulty keeping pace. The engine must have been modified.

"I'm losing him," he said to dispatch. And then he saw something he didn't expect. The SUV made a U-turn over the median despite traffic and honking horns. Most people had the sense to get out of the way, but the vehicle was heading right toward him. "Scratch that. He did an about-face."

Dawson ducked low as the driver fired at him. The bullet pinged the top of his truck missing the windshield but nailing the metal roof.

"Are those shots fired?" dispatch asked.

"Yes, they are." He filled her in on the SUV's new direction. "Heading southbound."

"Copy that."

The sound of a chopper roaring toward them clued Dawson in on the change in direction. The SUV weaved in and out of traffic before popping a curb and nearly wiping out a sidewalk full of people.

Folks scattered as the SUV came to an abrupt stop. From this angle, Dawson had to make a U-turn to see the driver's side but he'd bet money on the fact the guy just took off.

"I'm going on foot." He glanced up and then provided the street name before parking. He jumped out of his vehicle, caught sight of a guy full-on running, and gave chase.

Runner was fast. The man was in good shape. He also had a weapon and wasn't afraid to turn and shoot, which he did.

The bullet took a small chunk of brick out of one of the buildings they were cutting in between. It was a wild shot, far off the mark.

Weapon drawn, Dawson wouldn't risk injuring an innocent person. But he sure as hell wasn't letting Runner get away when he was this close.

This was the first mistake and real break in the case.

Staying back far enough for Runner not to be able to get off a good shot was key. Dawson could keep running for a long time without a break. He hoped Runner's stamina was weak.

Runner spun around and fired. Dawson flattened his back against the wall. He'd gotten a little too close for comfort that time, the bullet pinging a couple feet away. He muttered a curse and froze when he realized Runner had stopped.

This time, the man slowed down enough to take aim when he fired. Except nothing happened. Nothing but a click noise came out of the gun.

Dawson made his move. He charged toward Runner and dove at him, tackling him at the knees as he tried to turn and run. Pavement bit hard. Pain shot up Dawson's elbow where he took the brunt of the fall. That was going to leave a mark, he thought wryly.

The weapon in Runner's hand went flying. It was no good to him anyway unless he wanted to use the butt of it as a hammer against Dawson's skull. The thought probably occurred to Runner as his gaze seemed to search for something to use.

And because everything that could go wrong usually did, Dawson's weapon flew out of his hand, too.

His target spun like an alligator with prey in his mouth. Runner might be middle-aged, but he was in great shape. Dawson could almost hear the crack as his head slammed into the concrete alley. A raging headache would spoil the rest of his day. He tried to shake off the ringing noise in his ears as Runner's hands wrapped around Dawson's neck.

Oh. Hell. No.

Curling up in a ball, despite Runner's best efforts to stop him, Dawson launched the heel of his boot at Runner's chest like it was on a spring. Impact knocked Runner back.

Hard contact loosened the man's grip on Dawson's throat. He sucked in a burst of air just in time to stave off the dizziness threatening. He coughed the minute air hit his lungs. His throat burned. But he couldn't focus on that right now. Runner was scrambling to his feet and reaching for Dawson's Glock.

Chapter Twenty

Summer kept pressure on the wound as she and Marcy crouched down behind a dresser. Marcy had led them to the middle of the room and to a spot where there was heavy furniture.

The door opened when they'd barely had time to squat down. Since she didn't hear sirens right outside, she feared someone had been left behind to deal with her and Marcy.

Fear tried to clasp its icy talons around her chest and squeeze her lungs. She forced herself to breathe and prayed Marcy would stay quiet.

Whoever was in the shed was stealth. There was no sound and Summer couldn't tell if the person had just opened the door to see if anyone was inside.

The light flipped on and Marcy gasped. Their location had been compromised. Summer scrambled to move them to a new location. She needed to get them out of there. Being locked in the small space with a killer wasn't going to end well.

Marcy's wound started bleeding again and Summer was certain they were going to leave a trail of blood. Could she secure Marcy somewhere, maybe in an empty cabinet? Summer could draw attention to herself and then run out the door.

It was risky. There wasn't enough time to go through all the reasons this was a very bad idea. Or, map out all the ways in which this plan could backfire.

All she knew for certain was that if they stayed together, they would most likely die. Trying to move the both of them as a unit might be certain death. Marcy was getting weaker, slower. Her panic was setting in.

Then again, emergency workers would be there in a matter of minutes. A thought struck. Had the driver left the scene to throw law enforcement off the track?

Summer was grateful for Dawson as she helped Marcy move toward the far right corner of the building. He wouldn't be easily tricked and yet he had no idea what was going down.

Inside the small space that seemed to shrink by the minute, she'd never felt more trapped. She scanned the area, looking for any kind of hiding space for Marcy. She could give her the small handgun Dawson had left with Summer.

Summer's hands were shaky as it was. Marcy might be the steadier shooter.

Another wave of panic engulfed Summer when the light flipped off. Whoever was inside the shed seemed to have gotten his bearings and decided moving in pitch-black was his best option.

More of those icy chills raced down Summer's

back at the implication. It would also make identifying him that much more difficult should Summer and Marcy survive.

Another thought struck and it lit a fire deep in her belly. This could be the bastard who'd murdered her sister. At the very least, he was involved.

More of that white-hot anger licked through her as she placed the gun in Marcy's shaking hand in case things didn't go the way Summer planned. She felt around for a cubby space that she could tuck Marcy inside.

Waiting it out for emergency personnel who might show too late was not an option. Not when this guy was inside the building. Besides, EMTs could be shot on arrival.

Summer had no idea how it all worked or who would show up. She wasn't willing to risk her or Marcy's life to find out. With a deep breath, she helped Marcy into a small space before crawling away. She made sure to swipe her hands on the floor to mess up the dirt trail just in case this guy decided to use a light. Every cell phone had a flashlight app.

This guy might find them, and he might kill them, but she didn't have to serve both of them up on a silver platter.

Winding through the tall stacks of furniture, she ran her hand along the plastic wrapping. Moving from bundle to bundle, she tried to get her bearings. It didn't take long to realize she was completely turned around. She stopped and listened for signs of him breathing.

She couldn't see her own hand if she held it out in front of her face. Hope that she could find the exit fizzled.

And then Marcy screamed and fired a shot.

Summer's bearings came real quick after that. She oriented herself and immediately beat feet, backtracking to Marcy. She could only hope Marcy's aim was on point.

Then again, she might have panicked and gotten off a wild shot.

"Sandy!" Marcy screamed.

Adrenaline spiked. It wasn't good that Marcy just let the creep know there was another person in the room. Now he would expect her to show.

It didn't matter, because she heard the sounds of a struggle and more screaming came from Marcy. Summer had no choice but to get back to the corner as fast as she could.

Glorious sirens sounded right outside the shed, close enough to know that help was so near she could almost reach out and touch it. Marcy might not have any more time. Summer might be too late. But she had to try.

So, she kept moving toward the scuffle.

The door opened. Light peeked in and she saw Scrappy three feet in front of her. He'd pinned Marcy to the ground and was running his hand along the floor, no doubt trying to find the gun.

Summer launched herself on top of him, screamed at the top of her lungs for help, and dug her fingernails into his eyes.

The light flipped on as Summer continued to scream for help.

"Everyone step outside, hands up." An authoritative female voice made the demand.

"There's a gun. He's…he killed my sister…"

This wasn't the movies. No cop would risk their own life by running in blind.

Time was the enemy.

Scrappy refocused all his attention on Summer. He twisted around, his height and weight giving him an advantage. After a grunt, he knocked her flat on her back, but Summer kept digging her fingernails in his face anyway. She clawed at his cheeks when her hands slipped from his eyes.

Even if he killed her and got away, she'd have enough DNA underneath her fingernails for police to nail him. Justice would be served.

He drew back his fist and before he could get off a jab, she bucked and rolled. He regrouped a little too quickly as Marcy started kicking.

It gave Summer the advantage she needed to knock him off balance and roll away from him. Something hard dug into her left arm. She moved away enough to check. It was the gun. Her hands were no longer shaky when she thought about her sister's senseless murder.

Scrappy's hand gripped her shoulder and when he spun her around this time, he met the barrel of a gun. Using her thumb, she clicked off the safety.

"You better back up right now or they'll be scraping your brains off the ceiling," Summer said through clenched teeth.

His gray eyes widened in shock but he listened.

"Put your hands in the air," she demanded. That part of all cop shows rang true.

Scrappy's eyes darted from left to right, no doubt looking for an escape route.

"Don't even think about it. I'll shoot."

He seemed to debate that for a split second.

"Give me a reason," she said, not backing down an inch.

A female officer poked her head around one of the heavy chests.

"Drop your weapon," she demanded.

Summer had no plans to argue. She moved slowly so the officer would be clear on her intent, lowering the gun to the floor. "Can I move it away from him?"

"Slide it toward me," the officer said, her weapon trained on Scrappy.

Summer complied. "My friend was shot. She's bleeding pretty badly. Is there an ambulance? She needs medical attention right now."

Another officer rounded the other side of the stack of furniture. He didn't speak but his weapon was trained on Scrappy.

The door opened.

"My friend took off. He's a US marshal. Is he okay?" Summer was desperate for information about Dawson.

The first cop shook her head.

"Lace your fingers on top of your head," she said

to Scrappy. He placed his hands up and shot a go-to-hell look at Summer.

Officer number two moved in and took Scrappy down. In a half second, he was face down chugging dust through his nose and out his mouth.

"I'm certain this guy was involved in my sister's murder." Summer realized that her nose was bleeding. "And he hurt my friend."

Marcy was sitting up, hands in the air.

"She needs medical attention," Summer repeated just as EMTs arrived on the scene.

The female officer patted down Summer and then Marcy. She signaled for waiting emergency workers to go ahead and treat the patient.

Within minutes, Marcy's bleeding had stemmed and she was being carried out of the building. Summer followed outside to the waiting ambulance.

"I'll come to the hospital as soon as I can," Summer said, praying she wouldn't be visiting two people in there.

Marcy grabbed hold of Summer's hand.

"You've got this. You're going to be okay. This is just a speed bump," Summer reassured.

Marcy squeezed Summer's hand and smiled through the oxygen mask.

"Sorry, ma'am. We've gotta roll," one of the EMTs said.

"I'll see you soon," she said to Marcy, who nodded.

Summer took a step back and watched as Marcy was loaded into the ambulance, the doors closed and one of the men in uniform bolted around to the driver's side. Lights on, the ambulance took off.

She reminded herself that Marcy was in good hands then turned to the female officer to give her statement.

"Is there a way you can check on my friend the marshal?" she pleaded with the officer, who was beginning to realize Summer wasn't a threat.

The officer nodded and spoke low into her radio, and then she listened. "Ten-four. Thank you."

"What is it?" Whatever was going on didn't sound good.

"Marshal O'Connor was involved in a vehicle chase. The suspect abandoned his vehicle and Marshal O'Connor pursued him on foot. Witnesses near the scene reported shots being fired. The whereabouts of the suspect and Marshal O'Connor are unknown at this time."

Summer's legs turned to rubber and she had to take a step back until she found the golf cart to keep herself upright. She leaned against the solid vehicle with the feeling that it was the only thing connecting her to Dawson.

"I'm sorry, ma'am." The officer was short, five feet three inches if Summer had to guess. Her long black hair was in a braid that ran halfway down her back.

Although she might be tiny, Summer had no doubt the woman could take care of herself.

"I'll need to take your statement if you want to

help the marshal." The officer was sympathetic. "I'm Officer Williams."

She stuck out her hand.

"Summer Grayson." She took the offering.

Officer Williams looked Summer up and down, focusing on the bloodstain on her pale blue shirt. "Do you need medical care?"

"It's Marcy's blood, not mine. Other than a bloody nose, I'm not hurt." Summer scanned her body just to be sure. There were going to be a few bruises but nothing that a warm bath and some antibiotic ointment couldn't handle.

"Okay. Start from the beginning and tell me everything that happened." Officer Williams pulled a notepad out of her pocket along with a small pen.

Summer relayed everything that had happened since they showed up at the apartment complex. "Dawson." She flashed eyes at the officer. "Marshal O'Connor wrote down the description Marcy provided. Matt visited my sister's things and most likely took evidence if my sister had any against him."

Officer Williams nodded as she jotted down key words along with the description.

Minutes ticked by with no word on Dawson or the guy he'd abandoned his truck to chase. Summer could barely breathe.

DAWSON TIGHTENED HIMSELF into a ball and rolled back onto his shoulders. Lifting his lower back off the ground, he sprang to his feet in a martial arts kip-up maneuver. He didn't have time to thank his training when he landed on his feet and in ready position. Runner's hand was within inches of the Glock.

He plowed into Runner, closed his arms around the guy's midsection like a vise, and rolled forward, bringing Runner with him. Dawson dug his fingers into the man's ribs before tucking and rolling.

Runner practically howled in pain.

Unwilling to let up or give the man an inch, Dawson rolled them both onto their sides and wrapped powerful legs around his target in a scissor leg lock. Runner squirmed and tried to break free from Dawson's grip.

Not this time.

Runner twisted and turned, and Dawson squeezed harder, waiting him out. The saying, patience won wars, was as true in hand-to-hand combat as it was in any battle.

Adrenaline would fade and, at this pace, Runner would deplete his energy. Both were already heaving for air. Dawson made a point to slow his breathing so he could control his racing pulse.

The struggle started to ease, and Dawson tightened his grip even more. This was where his endurance training would kick in and he damn sure needed it.

Dawson managed to wrangle one arm around Runner's elbow, locking it into place. The man was lying on his other arm, rendering it useless. There was still a loaded gun in the vicinity and Dawson couldn't risk Runner getting to it first.

Reaching back, Dawson felt around for his Glock.

He knew it was close behind him. He just didn't know how close.

Arching his back, he reached a little farther. Unfortunately, the move gave Runner enough room to break his elbow free. He jabbed it into Dawson's chest, knocking the air from his lungs.

Well, that just angered him even more.

Dawson bucked as his hand landed on the butt of his weapon. The cold metal felt good in his right hand. He spun around onto his back, bringing Runner with him. The move freed his right hand to bring the Glock up to Runner's temple.

"Go ahead. Make another move. Flinch the wrong way and this is all over. I'll put a bullet through your skull." The last thing Dawson wanted was to give this guy the easy way out with death.

"Don't do that." Runner grunted, his muscles stiffening. "I can explain this whole mix-up."

Mix-up? Dawson grunted.

Runner, whoever the hell he was, needed to serve his time and spend the rest of his freakin' life locked behind bars. It was the only way to bring justice to Cheryl, Autumn and their families.

Despite what Summer had said, Autumn had family. She'd had her sister and no O'Connor would've turned their back on her. She'd become part of the family, a rare club that took care of its own. Her legacy was complicated, but that didn't mean she didn't have family.

Tying this bastard to the crimes was another story altogether. A slick guy like this would lawyer up.

Running away from a crime scene wasn't exactly the same as murder.

"Roll over onto your stomach and keep your hands where I can see them at all times," Dawson instructed.

Runner did.

"Hands behind your back." Gun trained to Runner's temple, Dawson rolled onto his side and then he sat up on his knees.

He was winded, but that didn't stop him from pulling zip cuffs from his back pocket and tying up Runner's hands. He patted the man down next and felt in his pocket for a wallet or some form of ID. There were no other weapons. All Runner had on him was a money clip with close to a thousand dollars in mostly hundred-dollar bills.

It figured there'd be no ID. If Dawson had to guess there wouldn't be anything tying the SUV back to this guy, either. He was smooth. This had been well thought out. And it might've worked against a civilian.

"What's your name, sir?" Dawson knew to dot every i and cross every t when it came to this guy. There was no way he was making a mistake that could cost the case.

When Runner didn't answer, Dawson identified himself one more time as law enforcement before Mirandizing him.

Chapter Twenty-One

Backup arrived.

Dawson had never been so happy to see fellow law enforcement officers. And they came running. A pair who looked opposite in every way possible came bolting toward him and Runner.

"Marshal O'Connor, sir, I'd be honored to help you with this suspect," the first one said. He was on the short side. Dawson would guess him to be in his early twenties. What he lacked in height he made up for in brawn. He had the body of a world-class gymnast. His nameplate read Smith.

"Be my guest." Dawson moved back enough to lean the back of his head on the nearest building to try to catch his breath. Every place he'd been kicked, punched or jabbed was waking up, making its presence known, bringing all kinds of pain to the forefront. He couldn't focus on any of that right now. "I had to leave behind my…" Words failed him on exactly how to describe his relationship to Summer. He decided on, "Girlfriend and an office worker at an apartment complex. One of them was shot and I don't know how bad the injury is. Do you—"

The second officer, Jenkins, was tall with dark skin and a mustache. He was nodding his head. "We've been following along on the radio. One of the victims was taken to the hospital by ambulance, the GSW. The other is giving her statement to a colleague, Officer Williams."

"Is there a way I can talk to her?" Dawson needed to hear Summer's voice. For reasons he couldn't explain, he needed to know she was all right. *Hells bells, O'Connor.* The reason was obvious. He loved her. He wanted to know she was all right because the thought of losing her knocked him in the chest so hard he couldn't breathe.

"I can call Officer Williams," Jenkins offered.

Dawson nodded.

"What's your name, sir?" Officer Smith asked Runner.

Apparently, the guy was invoking his right to remain silent.

"He didn't talk for me, either," Dawson said as he watched Jenkins make the call.

When the officer turned the phone over, Dawson immediately listened for Summer's voice.

"Dawson, are you there?" Her voice was like velvet.

"I'm here." He took a second to breathe as relief flooded him. Hearing her voice set things right inside him that he didn't realize had been broken. "I heard Marcy's on her way to the hospital."

"She looked pretty bad, Dawson. There was so much blood and then the skinny guy from—"

"Hold on a second. What skinny guy?" All his internal alarm bells sounded. The thought he'd left them alone and vulnerable tightened the knot in his gut. And then it dawned on him who she was talking about. The two guys who'd chased her were nicknamed Scrappy and Thick Guy. "The one from a few days ago?"

"Yes—"

"Are you hurt?" Fire raged through him at the thought.

"No. I'm okay. A couple of bumps and bruises, a bloody nose… I'm just worried about Marcy. She lost a lot of blood."

"I'll pick you up as soon as I'm cleared here. Did they say which hospital she was going to?" he asked.

"No. I forgot to ask. The EMTs got going with her really fast. She was so pale," she said, and he heard the worry in her voice.

"I can find out. I'm on my way to my vehicle right now." He pushed up to standing. "I'll see if an officer can stay with you until I get there."

"Okay." There was hesitation in her voice. This wasn't the right time to tell her how he felt about her. Not while Marcy was in a hospital fighting for her life. "Dawson…"

"Yeah?"

"I—uh…never mind. I guess I'll see you in a few minutes," she said. He needed to ask what that was all about but everything could wait until they got a status update on Marcy.

Plus, he needed to get to her. He needed to hold her in his arms. He needed to be her comfort.

And he hoped like hell she needed the same from him.

"I'll be there as fast as I can." Dawson had caught his breath and his truck was in good shape. He could jog back to his ride and get to her inside of fifteen to twenty minutes if the roads were clear.

"I'll see you soon." Summer ended the call.

Dawson turned to Officers Jenkins and Smith. "Can you guys handle this from here? I need to pick up my...*someone* and get her to the hospital to check on our friend. I'll be there for a little while if you want to swing by for my statement. Or, I can come down to the station."

Jenkins was already shaking his head.

"No, sir. You go take care of your *friend.* We got this suspect from here."

"Thank you." He'd never meant those pair of words more. He took off back toward his truck and started feeling the effects of the fight with Runner.

This guy refused to identify himself. He carried no ID. One look at him said he had plenty of money to smooth over any bumps in the road.

The fact the evidence against him was all circumstantial burned Dawson's gut. A sympathetic jury pool would acquit in a heartbeat. If the runner was powerful enough to have a detective leave her job and someone killed in county lockup, he could find a way out of this.

Dawson made it to his vehicle, thankfully right where he left it. He fished keys out of his pocket and slid into the driver's seat. He navigated back onto the road and backtracked using his GPS.

His pulse galloped the entire ride back to the apartment complex. He pulled up to the scene where a female officer stood outside her squad car, arms folded as she talked to Summer.

The second Summer locked gazes with him, she started toward him. He didn't bother parking, he just stopped in the middle of the lot. He wasn't concerned about turning off his truck, either.

All he wanted was to feel Summer in his arms where she belonged. Dawson had never felt home in another person before Summer.

And the world righted itself for just a moment when she buried her face in his chest. He looped his arms around her and she pressed her body flush with his.

This was what love was supposed to be. Not obligation. It was supposed to feel like this, like he didn't want to spend another day without her in his arms.

Even though she'd ran straight to him and held on to him like there would be no tomorrow, he had no idea if she needed a friend or if she needed him. Big difference.

Dawson would take whatever she was willing to give. But first, they had to get to the hospital and check on Marcy.

Officer Williams walked over and introduced her-self. Dawson thanked her for staying with Summer.

"You're welcome, sir. It's a pleasure to meet you." Officer Williams had stars in her eyes when she looked at him. Other departments gave him a healthy amount of respect and he appreciated them for it. His division prided themselves on cooperating with other agencies and it had bought them a helluva lot of good will over the years.

"Take care," he said as he walked with Summer to the truck. She climbed in on the driver's side and scooted to the middle of the bench seat. She seemed to need physical contact as much as he did. He hoped that was a good sign.

He also had bad news to deliver but that could wait until they checked on Marcy.

THE HOSPITAL WAS a ten-minute drive that took twenty in traffic. Summer sat scooted up against Dawson, thigh to thigh. Her heart had fisted when she'd seen his face and then relief flooded her that they were both alive.

"I just realized something. We don't even know Marcy's last name," she said to Dawson.

He gripped the steering wheel as he navigated through the heavy traffic. "I can get us past the lobby with my badge. I'm guessing there aren't a whole lot of GSWs in the middle of the day at the hospital."

"GSW?" She had no clue what that meant.

"Gunshot wound." His reply was low and rev-erent.

"Oh." Those weren't exactly her favorite words to hear right now. Seeing the scared look on Marcy's face would haunt Summer long after this ordeal was over. She leaned into Dawson, drawing as much strength from him as she could. Her body started shaking and she imagined it was because her adrenaline finally wore off.

Exhaustion hit like a motorcycle going a hundred miles an hour and then slamming into a wall.

Dawson pulled into the ER bay and parked. He threw his shoulder into the door to open it and grunted. She realized he must've taken a few blows. His face was perfect unlike hers. Officer Williams had given Summer a few wipes while they waited for Dawson.

Summer was able to wipe off the blood, but her busted lip couldn't be cleaned so easily. That was sticking around.

He opened the door before helping her step out of the truck. As soon as her shoes hit concrete, he blew out a breath and then kissed her. His lips were gentle on hers but that didn't mean there wasn't a sizzle below the surface.

He locked gazes, holding for just a few seconds before linking their fingers together and heading inside the ER.

With his free hand, he pulled out his wallet and flashed his badge. "You had a GSW come in during the last hour via ambulance."

The nurse at the intake station was already nodding her head. "There's a waiting room through those doors, all the way down the hall and to the left. I'll update the file to let the doctor know you're waiting."

"Thank you," was all Dawson said before heading down the hall.

The waiting room was small. There were only about a dozen chairs. Everything was blue. The chairs, the carpet, the curtains. The wallpaper had hints of blue. None of which mattered because all she cared about was Marcy being well cared for.

There was coffee. She and Dawson seemed to notice it at the same time because they both made a move in that direction.

He poured two cups and handed one over. She took a few sips, welcoming the burn on her throat.

"Do you want to sit or stand?" he asked.

"I'm not sure my legs can hold me up much longer." She wasn't kidding. The past few days had caught up to her and she could barely stand. She also glanced down at her shirt and realized she must be a sight.

A nurse stepped inside the room and identified herself as Ramona. She was late thirties, with kind eyes and a round face.

"I brought you something to change into if you'd like," she said to Summer, holding out a shirt that looked like scrubs.

"Thank you." Summer took the offering and hit the bathroom. She washed off more of the blood and splashed cold water on her face.

"She's in surgery but the outlook is good," Dawson said as soon as Summer returned. Ramona had already left.

"That's great news." Summer reclaimed her seat and took another sip of coffee, anything to wake her up.

He nodded. Then said, "There's not so good news about the case."

Dawson's serious expression sent a wave of panic rippling through her.

"What is it?" Bad news only got worse with age.

He explained the situation with the guy he called Runner, and her heart literally sank.

"Marcy can ID him. He came to the apartment complex to go through my sister's personal belongings," she said.

"Won't make a difference. It's all circumstantial evidence. We don't have anything directly linking this guy to the murders. Our Runner did try to kill a US marshal and that should be enough to jail him for a long time. And Scrappy tried to kill Marcy and Summer. The police officers in the shed are witnesses, as well." There was so much frustration in his voice. "With a good lawyer, he could get out of jail in a few hours."

"Even though he shot at a US marshal?"

"Trust me, an expensive lawyer could create doubt." Dawson issued a sharp sigh. "That's how the legal system works."

"Well, that's messed up."

"At times, it is. Most of the time, though, it works. That's why I still do this job," he explained.

"We need proof that he's tied to my sister or Cheryl." She sat up straighter and took another sip of coffee. It was strong and black.

"I'd hoped we would find something in your sister's personal effects."

"But he got there first." Of course, he had. The bastard.

Chapter Twenty-Two

Summer felt around in her handbag, needing to feel the necklace in her fingers and some connection to Autumn. A thought came to her. "My sister would've known him well enough to realize he'd go through her stuff at the apartment complex."

She pulled out the necklace and stared at it for a long moment.

Dawson's cell buzzed. He fished it out of his pocket and stood up. "This is Dawson O'Connor."

He paused for a long moment before saying a few uh-huhs into the phone. He thanked the caller and then ended the call. "The runner's name is Mateus Hank."

"Sounds a lot like Matt Shank." The wheels started spinning in Summer's head. "She left clues, Dawson. She wanted us to figure this out."

The cold metal warmed in her hand and she traced the letters with her index finger. Holding the necklace in her hand gave her an idea.

"What if she wasn't protecting me? What if my sister tucked this inside the box as a clue?" There was no need for coffee now with the way her mind clicked through theories.

"It's possible." He nodded. "But where does the clue lead?"

"I don't know yet. My first thought is the place where we bought these. The fairgrounds." She flattened out her palm and looked at the dull piece of metal. "I can't let that bastard walk away scot-free."

"Agreed."

The door to the waiting room opened and a man in scrubs walked inside. He was average height with a runner's build and a full head of gray hair. "Good afternoon, my name is Dr. Warner."

Dawson stood and Summer followed suit. Each shook the doctor's hand.

"Your witness is doing well. She's out of surgery now and did great." He went through the procedure using medical jargon that Summer couldn't understand if she'd tried. But she got the gist of what he was saying.

"We gave her a transfusion because she lost a lot of blood. All in all, we're expecting a full recovery. She'll be resting for a little while. We're keeping a close eye on her. No visitors for the next few hours until she gets out of ICU." He put a hand up to reassure them. "Out of an abundance of caution."

Dawson thanked the doctor. He reassured them, once again, that Marcy was expected to make a full recovery.

"I wish she had family here waiting for her," Summer said after he left.

"Her parents are being notified. I'm sure they'll

be here soon." He walked over to where they'd been seated and drained his coffee cup. "We have a couple of hours. Are you ready to hit the fairgrounds?"

"I'm ready to find evidence that will nail that bastard to the wall."

"That's my girl." Dawson seemed to catch himself on those last words. Her heart performed a little flip at the term of endearment.

She walked over to him and pressed up on her tiptoes. He met her halfway and their lips touched so gently it robbed her breath.

This time, she linked their fingers.

WALKING ONTO THE empty fairgrounds brought on a rush of memories. The smell of funnel cake. Livestock. The bright lights and all those carnival rides.

Autumn's favorite had been the Tilt-A-Whirl. Nothing said the fair like strapping themselves into a ride that spun so fast and hard they almost tossed up their candy apples.

Cotton candy. Autumn couldn't get enough of it. She was terrible at games but never passed one she didn't think she could win anyway. Her seven-year losing streak was always on the verge of being over, according to Autumn.

The fair was the one place they'd gone every year without fail. They laughed and played. They would feed llamas and pet baby pigs. For that one day, they weren't poor or hungry.

Tears welled at the memories.

Walking hand in hand, she led him to where she

remembered the necklace booth to have been. There wasn't much there now but a patch of grass. She looked around for a hiding place.

There was a light pole with a metal plate screwed onto the base. "Maybe in there, Dawson."

He'd brought a pair of gloves and a paper bag that he'd explained was used for collecting evidence. He'd grabbed a few other items that he explained were useful. Things like tongs.

Dawson moved over to the light pole and took a knee. He examined the plate. "There's a screw missing."

Her heart leaped in her throat at the possibility of this hunch panning out.

"It's loose." He jiggled the plate.

Chill bumps ran the length of her arms. Experience had taught her not to get too excited before she had something concrete but this was promising.

Somewhere deep in her gut, she knew that if her twin hid something anywhere that it would be here. She prayed someone else hadn't gotten to the evidence first.

Dawson snapped a few pictures of the plate from different angles. He pulled a screwdriver from his pack and went to work loosening the screws. He set the plate down carefully and shone a light inside the six-by-four-inch opening.

A small smile crept across his lips. Summer knew. There was something inside.

Using the tongs, he pulled out a freezer bag through the opening. He set it down and then checked for more. A second freezer bag came and then a third.

One of the bags contained what looked like a journal. It was labeled My Story.

The second bag was labeled Cheryl. It contained some type of bloody clothing along with pictures that had been taken of her after she'd been strangled.

In the final bag, there were pictures with labels on the backs.

Dawson flipped over the bag with the journal in it. There was a folded-up sheet of paper tucked in the back with Summer's name on it. He opened the bag carefully and, using the tongs, pulled out the note.

He set it down on the grass and smoothed it out for her to read.

Summer,
this is bad. I've gotten myself involved with a bad person and I don't know how to get out without him hurting the people I love. He's powerful and rich. And I just found evidence that he killed his last girlfriend, Cheryl. I put it in the bag with her name on it. I think he knows I've figured him out. He's been threatening to dig into my past and find all the dirt if the cops show. He's been to parties at the governor's house. He took me as his date. He can cover up anything he wants. His name is Mateus Hank and he's the CEO of some bank. Anyway, I think he has politicians in his pocket.

I can't risk him finding you. So, I have to figure something else out. I wish I could tell you about all this. But, knowing you, you'd just come here and get yourself in the same hot water I'm in.

I tried to get out with Dawson O'Connor. I thought he could keep me safe and I cared about him. No one can hide from Mateus for long. He knows too many people and I saw one of his friends at the O'Connor ranch. I knew then I had to get away from there or risk him getting hurt.

I have a lot of regrets, sis. I thought I could come back to Austin and handle Mateus. He says he loves me but it's not the good kind. Anyway, I have to go. Love you more than words.

Tears streamed down Summer's face as she read the note from her sister.

"Now we know. She said it herself. She collected evidence against him and probably threatened him. He knew she had something but he didn't know where," Summer surmised.

"He kills her and then you show up. He knows you are trouble for him so he hires thugs to take care of you," Dawson said. He glanced at the plastic bags. "These are proof. This is all we need to link him to the murders."

Summer took the necklace out of her purse and held on to it. Her sister had been protecting her all along.

AN HOUR HAD passed by the time the last officer had left the fairground. Summer looked up at Dawson as he walked over to her and pulled her into an embrace.

"Where do we go from here?" She realized this was the end of the road for them. There would be justice for Autumn and Cheryl. Her sister was gone. There was no reason to stick around Texas, except that she'd never felt more at home than since she'd been back.

"Look into corruption at Austin P.D. for one," he said. "Make sure the evidence is handled properly and justice is served."

"Agreed."

"I don't make rash decisions." Dawson looked into her eyes and her heart fluttered like a dozen butterflies were trapped inside her chest.

"Good. Neither do I."

"So, I've given this a lot of thought. Over the past few days, we've had a crash course in getting to know each other. I feel like we skipped over all the formalities and dove straight in with both feet. I got to know the *real* you."

She nodded. About the only thing she was certain of was that she didn't want to walk away.

"I have to caution you right there, Dawson. This is my heart we're talking about and I don't normally *do* trust. But the thought of things ending right here—"

"Who said anything about ending what we have?"

"Weren't you about to?" Her heart really worked overtime now.

"No. I was about to ask you to stay. I haven't done a great job of expressing it but I'm in love with you, Summer Grayson. I've never been in love with anyone before you and I promise to love you for the rest of my life if you'll have me." He got down on one knee. "So, I'm asking you to stay. I'm asking you to consider making what we have permanent and official because I don't want to spend another day without you in my life."

Happy tears rolled down her cheeks now.

"I love you, Dawson O'Connor. You're my family and the only home I've ever known. Of course, I'll stay. And I'll spend every day of the rest of my life loving you."

Summer pressed a kiss to Dawson's lips, tender but with the promise of passion. He pulled back enough to smile at her and her heart took another hit. She could look into those eyes forever.

"My beautiful Summer," he said against her mouth. "Let's check on Marcy and then go home."

Summer couldn't think of a better plan. She'd found home. And she was ready to get started on forever.

* * * * *

Look for the next book in USA TODAY
bestselling author Barb Han's
An O'Connor Family Mystery series
when Texas Law *goes on sale next month!*

And don't miss the previous title in the series:

Texas Kidnapping

Available now wherever Harlequin Intrigue
books are sold!

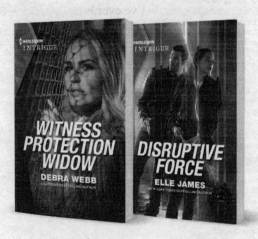

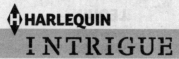
#1965 TOXIN ALERT
Tactical Crime Division: Traverse City • by Tyler Anne Snell
After a deadly anthrax attack on Amish land, TCD's biological weapons expert Carly Welsh must work with rancher Noah Miller to get information from the distrustful members of the community. But even their combined courage and smarts might not be enough against the sinister forces at work.

#1966 TEXAS LAW
An O'Connor Family Mystery • by Barb Han
Sheriff Colton O'Connor never expected to see Makena Eden again. But after she darts in front of his car one night, the spark that was lit between Makena and Colton long ago reignites. With a rogue cop tracking them, will they walk away—together?

#1967 COWBOY UNDER FIRE
The Justice Seekers • by Lena Diaz
Following the death of her friend, Hayley Nash turns to former cop Dalton Lynch for help. Dalton finds working with the web expert to be an exercise in restraint—especially when it comes to keeping his hands to himself.

#1968 MOUNTAIN OF EVIDENCE
The Ranger Brigade: Rocky Mountain Manhunt
by Cindi Myers
Eve Shea's ex is missing. Although her romantic feelings for the man are long gone, her honor demands she be a part of Ranger Commander Grant Sanderlin's investigation. But as more clues emerge, is Eve's ex a victim—or a killer targeting the woman Grant is falling for?

#1969 CRIME SCENE COVER-UP
The Taylor Clan: Firehouse 13 • by Julie Miller
Mark Taylor can put out a fire, but Amy Hall is a different kind of challenge. He's determined to keep her safe—but she's just as certain that she doesn't need his protection. As they hunt down an arsonist, will they trust each other enough to surrender...before a madman burns down their world?

#1970 THE LAST RESORT
by Janice Kay Johnson
When Leah Keaton arrives at her family's mountain resort, armed insurgents capture her, but Spencer Wyatt, the group's second in command, takes her under his protection. Spencer is an undercover FBI agent, but to keep Leah safe, he's willing to risk his mission—and his life.

Makena needed medical attention. That part was obvious. The
tricky part was going to be getting her looked at. He was still
trying to wrap his mind around the fact Makena Eden was
sitting in his SUV.

Talk about a blast from the past and a missed opportunity.
But he couldn't think about that right now when she was injured.
At least she was eating. That had to be a good sign.

When she'd tried to stand, she'd gone down pretty fast and
hard. She'd winced in pain and he'd scooped her up and brought
her to his vehicle. He knew better than to move an injured
person. In this case, however, there was no choice.

The victim was alert and cognizant of what was going on.
A quick visual scan of her body revealed nothing obviously
broken. No bones were sticking out. She complained about her
hip and he figured there could be something there. At the very
least, she needed an X-ray.

Since getting to the county hospital looked impossible at least in the short run and his apartment was close by, he decided taking her to his place might be for the best until the roads cleared. He could get her out of his uncomfortable vehicle and onto a soft couch.

Normally, he wouldn't take a stranger to his home, but this was Makena. And even though he hadn't seen her in forever, she'd been special to him at one time.

He still needed to check on the RV for Mrs. Dillon…and then it dawned on him. Was Makena the "tenant" the widow had been talking about earlier?

"Are you staying in town?" he asked, hoping to get her to volunteer the information. It was possible that she'd fallen on hard times and needed a place to hang her head for a couple of nights.

"I've been staying in a friend's RV," she said. So, she was the "tenant" Mrs. Dillon had mentioned.

It was good seeing Makena again. At five feet five inches, she had a body made for sinning underneath a thick head of black hair. He remembered how shiny and wavy her hair used to be. Even soaked with water, it didn't look much different now.

She had the most honest set of pale blue eyes—eyes the color of the sky on an early summer morning. She had the kind of eyes that he could stare into all day. It had been like that before, too.

But that was a long time ago. And despite the lightning bolt that had struck him square in the chest when she turned to face him, this relationship was purely professional.

Don't miss
Texas Law *by Barb Han,*
available December 2020 wherever
Harlequin Intrigue books and ebooks are sold.

Harlequin.com

Get 4 FREE REWARDS!

We'll send you 2 FREE Books plus 2 FREE Mystery Gifts.

Harlequin Intrigue books are action-packed stories that will keep you on the edge of your seat. Solve the crime and deliver justice at all costs.

FREE Value Over **$20**

Love Harlequin romance?

DISCOVER.
Be the first to find out about promotions, news and exclusive content!

Facebook.com/HarlequinBooks

Twitter.com/HarlequinBooks

Instagram.com/HarlequinBooks

Pinterest.com/HarlequinBooks

ReaderService.com

EXPLORE.
Sign up for the Harlequin e-newsletter and download a free book from any series at **TryHarlequin.com**

CONNECT.
Join our Harlequin community to share your thoughts and connect with other romance readers!
Facebook.com/groups/HarlequinConnection